ALASKA HIGHWAY ADVENTURE SERIES

Volume 1

THE GLADSTONE LAKES MYSTERY

DAVID SKIDD

MIDNIGHT INK

Published by Midnight Ink, Palm Desert, California

ISBN: 0-9636214-0-8

First Midnight Ink printing May, 1993
Revised edition, February, 1995

Printed in the U.S.A.

THE GLADSTONE LAKES MYSTERY

Contents

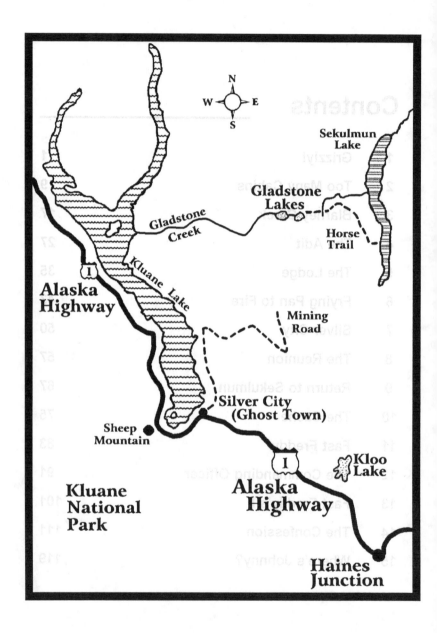

1

GRIZZLY!

On their third day in the Yukon Territory, Jonathan and Ashley were playing horseshoes when their younger brother Matthew returned to camp.

"Hi, guys. I'll play the winner," said Matthew, flopping at the base of a pine tree.

Startled, Ashley spun in his direction. "Matthew Adams, you must be half cat the way you move so quietly. I'm worried about bears and you creep up without a sound. Please don't do that while we're here. *Please!*"

"Chill, Ash...I'm sorry. I should wear a bear bell so you can hear me coming." He paused, averting his sister's eyes. He didn't want to get her upset. She was more or less in charge and he wanted to stay on her good side. He tried changing the subject. "This is such a cool place. Why don't people live here year round?"

"Dad says it's too cold in winter," said Jonathan, lining up a toss. "Plus, you can't get farther away from the rest of the world than here. That's why I like it. We're so far from everything. California doesn't seem to exist." With that, he tossed a ringer. "I win!" he exclaimed, jabbing the air with his fist. "The guys win again...who'll be the next victim of the Sekulmun Lake champ?"

Ashley was about to point out she'd won the previous four games when she suddenly stiffened.

"Quiet," she whispered. "Listen. Over by the fuel barrels...something's moving. Jonathan, if it's a bear..."

Jonathan heard a rustling sound, like a tree branch brushing the side of a house. "There's something there, all right. We'd better think fast. We're too far from the cabin...what would Dad do...?"

Matthew was frozen by fear. Ashley broke the paralysis.

"Move it," she whispered. "We can't just stand here."

They tried to listen, think and see all at once.

"The tree!" cried Jonathan. "Up the tree!"

They ran to a nearby pine tree. Whatever was moving near the fuel barrels now knew it had company.

"Climb, Matthew," ordered Jonathan. *"Hurry!"*

Matthew stepped into Jonathan's clasped hands and scrambled up the tree. The bark cut his hands, but his legs and arms felt like they were nuclear powered.

In moments they were high above the ground. Ashley scanned the area below, but she was shaking and her eyes couldn't focus. She tried to calm down as the adrenalin kept pumping.

2

"I don't know if you can see, but don't fall," said Matthew. "Th...th...there's a bear and he...he...he's..." His voice trailed away.

Ashley watched the huge bear move toward the tree. She zoned out, hypnotized by his menacing presence. Years of training in wilderness survival hadn't prepared her for the reality of a grizzly coming at her. Her life was over, about to be terminated by a gang of one. He would break the tree with his powerful paws and attack.

"Why?" she asked. "Why did we come here where animals attack people and get away with it, where there's no one to call for help, no 911? This isn't fair." Her home in California flashed in her mind's eye. She knew she would never swim in her pool again, never relax in the hot tub, never see her friends again.

"Never...never...never!" she screamed at the bear. *"Never...never...never!"*

The bear shook the tree with his paws. He grunted — a deep *woof.* Backing up, he shook his head from side to side. Then he stood motionless, gazing at the tree, waiting. Suddenly, the bear turned and lumbered into the forest. In seconds he was gone. Ashley and her brothers gripped the branches, watching their worst nightmare walk away. They were still too frightened to breathe.

A warm breeze shaped riffles on the lake. High above, a bald eagle demonstrated gliding maneuvers to her awkward offspring. Silence settled around the pine tree. A mile away, the king of this wilderness moved through the evergreens, satisfied he had asserted his authority.

THE WOODPECKER'S SECRET

Now they faced a new fear — fear of the unknown. The color had drained from Matthew's face and Jonathan knew he needed reassurance.

"Yo, Matt. Did you see that dude?" Jonathan knew there was no guarantee the bear would leave them alone, even though he was out of sight. But they couldn't stay in the tree forever. "We have to get out of this tree."

"Maybe we should wait until Dad gets back," suggested Matthew. "He said he might only be gone for three days."

"Three *minimum*," said Ashley. "More like five or six. We have no choice. We have to get to the cabin." Their father, a heart surgeon, had left camp the previous evening to deal with an emergency.

"Ashley," suggested Jonathan, "let's give Mr. Griz time to get away and we'll run for the cabin. Do we go together or one at a time?"

"Together!" blurted Matthew. He wasn't interested in running to the cabin alone. "We go together."

Ashley laughed. "We'll go together, we'll go together, Matthew." She began to descend. At the lowest branch, she still had a big drop to the ground. She wondered how she got up in the first place. Hanging momentarily from the branch, she let go, landing with a *thunk*. She waved the others down. "Let's go. We may not have much time."

Jonathan climbed down. Once on the ground, he looked out for Matthew while Ashley watched for the bear. "Matthew, what are you doing? Come on. Look at him,

Ashley. He's going up the tree. Matthew, are you crazy? The bear might...we have to get to the cabin."

Matthew had done this before. If he wanted to do something, nothing would stop him. Sometimes he even ignored his father, which got him in deep trouble. The bear wasn't even a memory as he moved from branch to branch — *up* the tree.

"There's a hole in the trunk," shouted Matthew. "A woodpecker's nest. There's something inside...hey... there's a baby! Come and see."

The twins sighed and looked at each other in resignation. The bear did seem to be gone and they knew Matthew was going to do what he wanted.

"When you're finished playing, let us know and we'll stroll to the cabin together," said Ashley. "No need to rush."

Her sarcasm was wasted. Matthew knew they were in danger but he wanted to see the nest. The little bird peeped. Maybe he thinks I'm his mother, thought Matthew. Then something in the nest caught his eye.

"Hey, there's something here...a pouch, nailed inside." He reached in and grasped the object. It *was* a pouch. "It's a pouch. It's a pouch! I found a pouch in the nest." He sat on a branch and turned the package over in his hands, studying it from every angle.

Jonathan and Ashley forgot the bear. They wondered why there was a pouch in a woodpecker's nest in a remote part of the Yukon Territory. How did it get there?

5

THE MESSAGE

They were perplexed. On the table lay a paper that had been tucked neatly inside the pouch. For hours they puzzled over the strange symbols, symbols they were certain contained a secret message.

1944

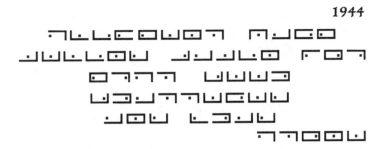

"Well, Matt," said Jonathan, putting a piece of wood in the stove, "we'll rely on you to break the code. You're always doing puzzles."

Matthew was concentrating and hardly heard his brother. He was lost in mental space, where he felt most comfortable. Here he was free to put information together, to devise ways of understanding puzzles. To Matthew, life was like an arcade game, a challenge to be mastered. First he had to learn the rules and then he had to put the pieces together. He was good at putting things together, but the rules of his life seemed to keep changing — as though a mad programmer kept reprogramming the game.

"It's a cipher, not a code. A cipher replaces each letter

with a specific character. I think this is an *E* and this one is probably an *A*. I'm sure I've seen this cipher before, but I can't remember..."

Ashley and Jonathan were silent. Their excitement had dwindled when they couldn't crack the code. Now, however, a feeling of expectation returned as their brother's agile mind clicked across his memory banks.

"The Civil War...it has something to do with the American Civil War. That's it! It's a cipher used by Union soldiers held in Confederate jails. I remember now. I have it. I think I can do it."

A B C	D E F	G H I
J K L	M N O	P Q R
S T U	V W X	Y Z

"See?" said Matthew. "If a box has four sides with a dot in the center, it's an *N*. If it has two sides, a bottom and a dot on the right, it's an *F.*" He drew a grid and placed the letters of the alphabet in the boxes. Before the twins realized how he was doing it, Matthew deciphered the message. The words appeared as though by magic.

"Awesome," breathed Ashley. "A real secret message. I wonder what it means?"

1944

SHIPMENT WARM
BEHIND CABIN YOU
MUST FEEL
FLATTERED AND GLAD
STONE

"It's about a shipment," said Jonathan, "but that could be anything."

Matthew wasn't thinking. He was tingling with the feeling you get when you do something exciting or important. His mind told him *he* had found the hidden pouch and discovered the meaning of the message. It was a delicious feeling.

"Matthew...Matthew," said Ashley, gently shaking his shoulder. "Little brother, are you home?" She knew he was in his own world, but she was too excited to let him dream. They had a secret message to figure out.

"I'm here," he said. "This is really hot. Dad will be impressed when he sees this. We've found treasure!"

Jonathan and Ashley smiled. This was Matthew's usual approach, always jumping to conclusions.

"Matthew, there are quite a few old cabins around here. We might not find a hidden shipment easily," said Ashley.

"We'll find it," insisted Matthew. He made his hand into a fist and poked the message as if threatening it. "We're going to find the treasure. We just *have* to."

8

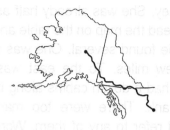

2

TOO MANY CABINS

I t was midnight and disappointment set in. They had searched behind their cabin and found only trees. To one side was a corral where horses were kept during hunting season and to the other was an outhouse. In front lay a sandy beach and Sekulmun Lake.

"We should eat and get some sleep," suggested Ashley. "We're not going to find anything tonight."

She was right. With all the excitement, they hadn't eaten since lunch, and the thought of food started them back to the cabin. Once inside, Jonathan cooked spaghetti while the others sprawled on their bunks.

"We should look at our topographical map," said Matthew. "It has cabins marked on it with red squares. Where's that map?" He rummaged through their supplies.

"On the shelf by the door, Matthew...not in the food

box," said Ashley. She was already half asleep.

Matthew spread the map on the table and looked for the red squares. He found several. One was across the lake and north a few miles. To the east was a lake called Aishihik and it had a dozen cabins along its shores.

His heart sank. There were too many cabins. The message could refer to any of them. Worse, most of the cabins were inaccessible except by float plane.

"What a downer. There are too many to check. We can't even get to most of them. Man, this bums me out. So much for our secret message." Disappointment filled Matthew's voice. He wasn't going to find treasure.

Jonathan didn't like seeing his younger brother unhappy. Their father noticed qualities in people he called special treasures. Matthew's special treasure was his enthusiasm and Jonathan wanted to give him a lift.

"Eat," said Jonathan. "If we can't find the hidden shipment, we can still go exploring. Maybe we'll get lucky." Matthew didn't respond.

"We could hike into the mountains," Jonathan persisted. "There's a horse trail from here to these two small lakes — Gladstone Lakes." He pointed to the map. "There's a cabin...we could go for the day. What do you say?"

"I suppose. Don't you think it's worth crossing Sekulmun Lake to the cabin on the other side?"

"We could," replied Jonathan. "But remember what Dad said about going out on the lake. Mr. Weatherby warned him this lake is dangerous because the wind comes up so fast. We don't know the lake and we could get in trouble."

Matthew knew what Jonathan meant. They could handle the boat, but Mr. Weatherby had told them a person couldn't last more than five minutes in the cold water of Sekulmun Lake. This wasn't southern California. "We'll go on a hike, then. But those lakes look far. Fifteen miles, I'd guess." He concentrated on the map, his enthusiasm returning. "We could take the tent and camp overnight. That would be fun."

"OK, we'll take the tent. We'd better check with Ashley, though. What do you think, Ash?"

Ashley was sound asleep. Her blond hair splashed across the pillow, framing her face. She looked like an angel.

THE HIKE

The next morning they filled their backpacks and set out for Gladstone Lakes. The boys convinced Ashley it would be safe to camp if they were careful. They carried bear flares, tubes the size of a pencil that shot bright flares into the air. The flares made a loud noise when fired and frightened bears away.

They carried a camping pot and enough food for several days. Most of the food was in foil pouches which they only had to heat in hot water. This was lighter than cans and animals couldn't smell food in sealed pouches.

The trail was easy to follow and provided good footing. It had been used by hunters for many years. Jonathan noticed the trees were smaller as they climbed into the mountains. Ashley thought it was because trees couldn't grow well where there was so little rain. Brightly-colored wildflowers, however, were everywhere. There were so many pink wild roses it felt like they were in a garden.

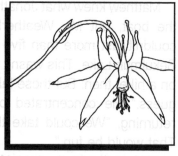

At a bend in the trail Jonathan halted. "Whoa," he said, stopping the others. "Look at that."

"Awesome," said Ashley. They were on a ridge high above a river that had carved its way through solid rock. From where they stood it was a straight drop of more than three hundred feet to the river's rushing water. Ashley gulped. "Excuse me, but how did we get *here?* I don't feel well." She stepped back. "This hike is over."

Jonathan and Matthew understood her reaction. The trail ahead was narrow and had a sheer vertical rock wall on one side and the white water below on the other. It didn't look like a horse would have room to walk.

"Maybe it's not so bad," said Jonathan. He wanted to be careful, but he also wanted to keep going. His father had taught him going forward was usually the best way to approach life. Retreating often left people feeling like they had missed something. "If hunters use the trail, it should be safe."

Ashley wasn't convinced. "We don't know where the trail goes, Jonathan. There may be rivers to cross."

"You're right. On the map it looks like we only cross

small creeks, but what's down there is no creek. If we have to cross, we'll turn back." Using binoculars, he tried to see where the trail was going. He couldn't tell. "We should keep going and see what we find," he concluded, handing the binoculars to Ashley. With an understanding twins share, he sensed she was ready to continue.

"This is great!" shouted Matthew, who had gone ahead.

They made their way along the cliff with the roar of rushing water rising from below. Several times the trail became very narrow and they walked hand-in-hand in single file. Soon the trail widened. They met small streams, but crossing was not difficult. Now and then they surprised a covey of grouse and they laughed as the birds flew with a *whoosh* into nearby trees to hide.

For no apparent reason, something suddenly came into Ashley's mind. "Jonathan, what's the name of the lakes we're going to?" she asked.

"Gladstone Lakes. Why?"

Ashley was visibly excited. "Matthew, come here. Where's the message? Let me see the message."

Matthew handed her the paper. "Just as I thought," she exclaimed. "Look at the last line."

1944

SHIPMENT WARM
BEHIND CABIN YOU
MUST FEEL
FLATTERED AND GLAD

STONE

The boys studied the message. Ashley realized they didn't get it. "What's wrong with you guys? Don't you see?"

"What, Ash?" asked Jonathan. "What are we supposed to see?"

"*Glad* and *Stone.* Gladstone Lakes...we're going to Gladstone Lakes!"

"*Cool!*" yelped Matthew. "You did it, Ashley. You did it! I thought *Stone* was the person who wrote the message. This is so radical. We're going to find treasure...we're going to find my treasure. Let's go. Gladstone Lakes, here we come."

Late in the evening they set up the tent. Ashley found a spot surrounded by pine trees where they felt safe. They built a campfire and cooked what Matthew called *cabbage rolls à la foil.*

Though the sun would be shining for several more hours, they were tired from the long walk. They sat by the fire talking about the secret message and Ashley's discovery of the word *Gladstone.* In spite of their excitement, drowsiness got the better of them and they crawled into their sleeping bags and were asleep before the sun set.

Matthew was up first in the morning. He lit the fire and

cooked breakfast for everyone. The aroma of food from the open fire made Ashley give up her struggle to sleep for five more minutes.

"This is going to be a great day," said Matthew. "Today we find the treasure of the Gladstone Lakes. Tonight," he continued, "we sleep on a bed of gold, surrounded by sparkling diamonds. I feel so hot." With that, he set off along the trail, leaving the twins shaking their heads in wonder.

Not far from their campsite, Jonathan and Ashley found Matthew crouched beside the trail. He held a finger to his lips. "See the marsh? There's something moving in the grass."

They crouched beside a tree, hearts racing. They hadn't forgotten the grizzly bear's visit at Sekulmun Lake. Jonathan reached for the binoculars and peered at the marsh. An animal emerged from the brush.

"What is it?" asked Ashley. She didn't think it was a moose, but she had never seen one so she wasn't sure. It had horns standing high above its head like a crown.

"Caribou," said Jonathan. "A woodland caribou. What a sight. He's looking around...he knows we're here."

Ashley took a turn with the binoculars and Matthew spotted more animals. "Look...there are more. There's a baby. A baby caribou!"

"I wish Dad could see this," said Ashley. "We should have brought the camera."

The animals *did* know they were being watched. All at once they started running away at high speed.

"What's happening?" asked Matthew. "Why did they take off so fast?"

"They smelled us," said Jonathan.

"You sure have a good eye, Matthew," said Ashley. "How did you see them? Maybe you could be a guide for Mr. Weatherby."

"Not me," said Matthew. "I wouldn't help people shoot animals. Dad said people who go with Mr. Weatherby want a trophy to put on their wall. Definitely not my bowl of sushi."

"Dad also said that by taking only a few animals each year, the herds stay healthy," said Ashley. "The animals have enough to eat if the herds don't get too big. Don't forget, Mr. Weatherby depends on the animals for his living."

"That's right," said Jonathan. "Most of Mr. Weatherby's customers only shoot animals with cameras and mount pictures on the wall. You could concentrate on guiding photographers."

Matthew wasn't sure what to think. He ran ahead, scouting for more caribou.

3

BLARNEY CREEK

After hiking for more than three hours, Jonathan began to wonder if they would ever reach the lakes. The trail went back and forth and it was hard to guess how far they'd walked. "Let's stop and eat," he suggested.

"I hear water," said Ashley. "Maybe we can find a nice spot by a creek."

They found the creek and took a break. As they relaxed, Ashley noticed something on a tree beside the trail. "It looks like a sign," she said, walking toward the tree.

She was right. The sign was rotten, but faint letters could be seen when she looked closely. "There's a B and an L and...I can't make it out. The second word looks like CREEK. That makes sense. It must be the name of this creek."

Jonathan joined her and tried to read the name. None of the small creeks on the map had names and he was surprised someone had named this one. "The last letter looks like a Y, and there's an R," he said.

"BLARNEY," exclaimed Ashley. "Blarney Creek."

"That's it," said Jonathan. "It must have been named by an Irishman."

"Excuse me," interjected Matthew, who remained seated on a log. "Believe it or not, we have company."

The twins turned sharply. "What?" they asked together. "Where?" They looked around, but saw nothing.

"Look up the hill, on the trail," said Matthew.

He was acting strangely...not like he would if he saw a bear. Then they saw the woman.

"Yo, what have we here?" she asked in a loud, sing-song voice.

The three were ready for almost anything, but not this. They wondered if their eyes were tricking them. The woman, in her thirties, was dressed in the finest hiking clothes a mail order catalogue could offer. Her hiking boots were new and expensive. The spotless safari jacket and pants had pockets everywhere. She wore an Aussie soldier's hat with a mosquito net draped over her face. Most striking was the wire leading from the bright tape player on her belt to the headphones on her ears.

"Hi! My name is Eloise," she said, jumping across the creek. "What are you doing here?"

They weren't sure if she was pleased to see them or not. Ashley introduced herself. "Hi. I'm Ashley Adams and

18

these are my brothers, Jonathan and Matthew."

"Oh, damn," swore Eloise, realizing she couldn't hear with the tape playing. She removed her headphones. "Now...what did you say?"

Ashley smiled. This was a strange lady. "I'm Ashley Adams and these are my brothers, Jonathan and Matthew," she repeated.

"A pleasure to meet you, Ashley. Are you kids with someone? I hope you're not in the wilderness alone — that would be a scandal. Do you realize there are wild animals in these woods? Last night at the Lodge we saw a *grizzly bear!* I didn't actually see it myself, but...in any case, you could get hurt."

"We're fine," said Matthew. "You're the one who should be worried. I wouldn't walk around here wearing head-phones."

Matthew caught Ashley's sharp look. Jonathan turned away, grinning.

"You're right," continued Eloise. "It's a bad habit. I'm from New York and I never go anywhere without my tapes. It shuts out the traffic noise, know what I mean? When I came here on the advice of my analyst, I missed the familiar sounds. It's so quiet here. So I thought...what the hell? It's good company." She flipped the cassette out of the machine and held it up. "At least I'm listening to the right stuff," she said, proudly.

Ashley couldn't believe her eyes. The name on the tape was *Soothing Outdoor Wilderness Soundtrack!*

"What's the deal with you kids, anyway? What are you

doing here?"

"What are *you* doing here?" shot back Matthew.

"Aren't you just the cutest little smartmouth?" she replied, pinching Matthew's cheek. "Like I said, my analyst figured I needed to get away from it all. He said I was working too hard. I'm a lawyer, and, well...what was I saying? Oh, yes," she continued, "I heard about this new Lodge in the Yukon Territory where there's real wilderness and *bam,* I'm on my way. That, short stuff, is why I'm here. Of course, the brochure did *not* mention the mosquitoes."

Matthew seemed to think he had found someone to talk to as an equal. "I haven't seen any mosquitoes," he said, turning to the twins. "Have you guys seen any mosquitoes?" They shook their heads.

"What? Are you kids jazzin' me? They're *everywhere!* I saw one only twenty minutes ago. It's disgusting. I hate bugs."

"Where's the Lodge?" asked Ashley. "We're looking for an old cabin on Gladstone Lakes. We didn't know about a Lodge."

Eloise calmed down. "The Lodge is about three miles back, on the lake. Actually, there are two lakes, and the Lodge is on the one farther away. I passed a cabin on my way here, on the second lake. But it's not old. Someone said it was a hunting cabin. If it is, I hope it burns down. Can you imagine letting people shoot wild animals in this day and age?"

She's a talking machine, thought Matthew.

"Last night we watched films of beautiful Dall sheep that live here. Of course, I haven't seen them in person because they stay on the tops of these mountains. I could have gone with a group today, but it sounded like work to me. You know, except for the bugs, I think the Yukon experience has really helped me. My analyst will be pleased."

Being from California, they had met strange people before. But they had never met anyone this strange. Jonathan wondered if all New Yorkers were like Eloise.

"It's been a slice rapping with you, but I'd better get back. It's a long walk, and mostly uphill." Eloise turned and headed back the way she had come. She wished them good luck before replacing the headphones and starting her tape machine. Then she was gone.

For a moment they stood watching her. Matthew started laughing, then Ashley, then Jonathan. Soon they were laughing so hard tears ran down their cheeks.

THE IMPORTANCE OF FLATTERY

The distance between Blarney Creek and the hunting cabin was shorter than expected. As an added surprise, the key to the lock on the Sekulmun Lake cabin fit the lock on the Gladstone cabin. Mr. Weatherby had said they could use any of his cabins, so they thought it would be all right to stay for a night as long as they left the cabin just as they found it.

Once organized, their conversation turned to the secret

message.

"This cabin is in the same place, relative to the lake, as the cabin on our map," said Jonathan. "But this can't be the cabin in the message because it's too new."

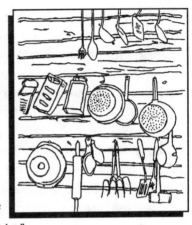

"Right," agreed Matthew. "Maybe we should look farther up the trail to see if we can find the original cabin."

"Maybe this cabin was built on the site of the old cabin," suggested Ashley. "If we can't find the original, we should assume this one replaced it."

"That would be a downer," complained Matthew. "There's no room behind this cabin to hide or bury anything." He was right. The cabin was built near the lake shore with the mountain rising directly behind it. There was very little room to bury anything. There were a few trees on the steep slope, but if anything was hidden there, it was more above the cabin than behind it.

"Let's go and take a look," urged Ashley, heading for the door. "I wonder if we'll meet more people from the Lodge?"

They investigated the area, searching for the original cabin. Nothing looked promising. Eventually they ended up at the Lodge. They didn't want to meet more tourists, so they stayed hidden in surrounding trees. They could see people in lounge chairs on the deck, but there wasn't much activity.

After a wide search, they were stumped. There was no old cabin. The only thing they found was a spring behind the new cabin, gurgling from the mountain and tumbling into the lake below.

They returned to the cabin and built a fire. Jonathan gathered and split some wood to replace what they used.

"You know," began Matthew, as he sat at the large table, "I still think there's a treasure. But I don't know what we should do next. I wish Dad could help us."

"Dad is probably in Sacramento operating on some senator's heart," said Jonathan. "I don't think I want to be a surgeon like Dad. He never gets time off. He can't even have a vacation."

Ashley disagreed. "He could have time off. He just works too hard, Jonathan. It's a question of what he chooses to do."

This was a discussion they'd had before. Usually Matthew only listened as the twins argued their points of view, but tonight he wanted them to stick to the subject he thought most important.

"Jonathan," he pleaded, "please check the message again to see if we missed something. You too, Ashley. We've come too far to just quit. We have to figure out the mystery."

"All right," agreed Jonathan. "If we can't figure it out, we can get Elegant Eloise to help us," he said, laughing.

"The words *flattered* and *warm* seem out of place," said

Ashley. "They may have a hidden meaning, like *glad* did."

"Maybe the spring behind the cabin has warm water," suggested Matthew.

"Could be," said Ashley. "We can check in the morning."

Jonathan began poking around the cabin looking for something.

"What are you looking for?" asked Matthew.

"A dictionary," replied Jonathan. "Probably a waste of time, though. Hunters don't use dictionaries." He pulled a box from under a pile of hunting magazines. "What do you know...a game." Opening the box, he found a tattered dictionary. "You never know what you'll find in a northern cabin," he said, flipping through the pages. "Here we are. *Flatter—Insincerely praise to gain some advantage.* Hmmm...not very helpful. What else can we look up?" He was about to turn the page when he stopped suddenly. His eyes grew wide.

"What is it?" asked Ashley. "What does it say?"

"It says," Jonathan continued slowly, "...*see Blarney Stone.* That's the name of the creek we stopped at today. Blarney Creek!" There was an electric feeling in the cabin as Jonathan turned to the *B's.* "Here it is. *Blarney Stone — Stone in Ireland traditionally kissed to gain skill in flattery.*"

"That's it!" exclaimed Ashley. "The shipment is near a rock at Blarney Creek."

"But the creek isn't behind the cabin," said Matthew. "The shipment can't be there *and* here. It doesn't make sense." Matthew was trapped between two emotions. He

24

was excited by the discovery, but was disappointed because the discovery didn't provide a logical explanation.

"Chill, Matt," cautioned Jonathan. "This is important. Maybe there's a cabin at Blarney Creek. We didn't look for one."

"That's a possibility," said Ashley. "The person who wrote this message was clever. He didn't intend it to be easy to find the shipment."

"Now we know what we'll do tomorrow," said Jonathan. "Right now, I'm going to bed. I don't know about you two, but I'm bushed."

The trio unrolled their sleeping bags on the bunks and fell asleep quickly.

Ashley heard the noise first. It was a scratching sound on the logs outside her window. She woke with a start when she realized what was happening. The scratching stopped. She waited, hardly breathing. She heard the noise again, louder this time.

"Jonathan," she whispered. "Jonathan."

Jonathan rolled over, but didn't wake up. Ashley could hear something, or someone, walking around the cabin. "Jonathan, wake up. There's something outside." This time Jonathan heard her.

"What's outside?" he whispered. He tried to adjust to the unfamiliar surroundings. Then he heard the noises. Something was pushing and scraping the cabin door. The racket became so loud even Matthew woke up.

"What's going on?" asked Matthew.

"Shhh," was Jonathan's reply.

The noise stopped again. Suddenly the window above Ashley's head shattered with a loud *crash.* She screamed at the top of her lungs. Jonathan leaped from his bunk and grabbed her arm, pulling her away from the window. Ashley was covered with glass.

Jonathan retrieved a flashlight from the table and ran to the window. There was no more noise. The flashlight's beam showed a shadow moving quickly through the trees away from the cabin. Though it was a moonlit night, Jonathan could only be sure that whatever the figure was, it was big.

4

THE ADIT

After the night's events, no one slept well. Late in the morning they decided to go back to Sekulmun Lake. They would search around Blarney Creek on their way. Before leaving, they boarded up the broken window.

"What kind of animal would break a window like that?" Ashley wondered aloud. "How many animals *could* break a window four feet above ground? It doesn't make sense."

"It's strange, all right," agreed Jonathan. "But bears often get into cabins and tear them apart. At least that's what Mr. Weatherby says. The problem is, the thing I saw running away didn't run like a bear."

"If it wanted to get in, why would it break the window and then run away?" asked Ashley.

"Ashley," said Matthew, "have you ever heard yourself

scream? Your scream is the eighth wonder of the world. That poor animal ran away because it thought a jet was going to land on its head."

Jonathan laughed. "He has a point, Ash. It's no mystery why it ran away."

Ashley blushed. She didn't see the humor. "Very funny." To herself she agreed the scream might have helped. "I guess we should go. It's a long walk back to Sekulmun."

Outside, they searched for clues.

"There are marks on the door," said Jonathan, "but I can't tell if a bear made them." The ground around the cabin was hard and covered with pine needles. Whatever visited had left no trace. They headed for Blarney Creek.

"Yo! What's this?" asked Matthew, picking something up. It was a piece of orange foam the size of a dime...it looked like a mushroom with no stem.

"A foam earphone cover," said Ashley.

"Like on Eloise's earphones," said Matthew. "It's the same color as hers."

"It's the same, all right," said Jonathan.

"What's it doing here?" asked Ashley. "We're not on the trail yet and I can't imagine Eloise going off the trail. Unless..."

"Unless she visited us last night," blurted Matthew. "This is where the thing ran. Maybe it wasn't an animal, after all."

"That would explain how the window was broken," said Ashley.

"It's as if she wanted to scare us away," said Matthew.

"But that doesn't seem right. She was so friendly. She didn't seem like a person who'd be out in the middle of the night. She might get dirt on her hiking boots," he said, grinning.

"This isn't funny, Matthew," said Ashley. "If she frightened us on purpose, it isn't one bit funny."

Matthew got the message. "OK, it isn't funny. But what can we do? Should we go to the Lodge and ask Eloise if she smashed our window?"

"No," said Jonathan. "What's the point? We might as well just go and look around Blarney Creek."

They took their time hiking to the creek, stopping to study animal tracks and chase a few grouse. At one point, Matthew thought he spotted a moose on a hillside. After watching for a while, they realized it was only dead tree branches that looked like moose antlers.

When they arrived at Blarney Creek, it looked the same as the day before. They couldn't find any big stone nearby that might give them a clue where to look for the shipment. After a short time only Jonathan kept searching. Matthew and Ashley sat on a log.

"Are you two going to sit there and let me do the work?" he asked.

"There's nothing here," replied Ashley.

"She's right, Jonathan," said Matthew. "You're wasting your time."

"Just sit there, then. But if I find the treasure, we agree it's all mine, fair enough?"

"No, you don't," said Matthew. "You can't pull that trick.

I'm still looking...only I'm doing it sitting down. We share the treasure."

"What treasure?" asked Jonathan, smiling.

Without realizing how his brother had tricked him, Matthew started searching again. "C'mon, Ashley, we'll show him who can find treasure."

A few minutes later Jonathan found what he was looking for. Not far from the trail was the side of a large hill. Where the creek flowed past the base of the hill, he climbed into a tangle of alders. It was hard to move through the branches and he could only see a few feet in front of him. His feet got soaked as he walked through piles of soft, damp moss.

He almost walked past the opening, but a piece of rotting timber jutted through the moss. It was big and looked out of place. He knew it meant there was an old mine nearby. A mine! What better place to hide a secret shipment? He searched for an opening in the side of the hill. He found another timber. Pushing through the thick brush, he finally found the opening.

"Ashley...Matthew! Come here. I found something." They ran toward the sound of his voice.

"Where are you?" cried Ashley. "We can't see you, Jonathan."

"In the alders," he yelled.

"What did you find?" asked Ashley, as she made her way to his side.

"I think it's a mine. This looks like the entrance."

Matthew's reaction was intense. "Radical. You found it,

Jonathan. You found the treasure!" He poked his head through the small opening in the side of the hill. "Whoa, this is spooky, man." He heard his words echo in the tunnel. *"...spooky...spooky."*

"It's an adit," said Jonathan. "That's what the entrance to a mine is called."

"Are we going in?" asked Ashley. "Do you think it's safe?"

"I don't know," replied Jonathan. "It's old. We're asking for trouble if we go in."

"Treasure," corrected Matthew. "We're asking for *treasure.*" He said the word like a thirsty person begging for water.

"Matthew," said Ashley, "we should think this over. If we were with Dad, would we go into an old mine? I doubt it."

Matthew felt the chill of meltdown. When Ashley looked after him when he was young, he could only act up a certain amount before she put him to bed. The point where she wouldn't change her mind was meltdown. He could hear it in her voice now.

"Ash," he said, deciding to go on offense, "Dad *isn't* with us. I think we should look inside. If it's too dangerous, we'll turn back." They were at a turning point. Without the secret message, they wouldn't even think of going into the old mine. The problem was, they *did* have the secret message.

"I'll go first," said Jonathan. "We'll be careful. If we see anything dangerous, we'll leave. OK, Ash?"

Ashley knew they really wanted to go into the mine. She

knew she wanted to go, too. She could hear her father's words: *Seize the moment!* She nodded in agreement. "Let's go for it."

With Jonathan leading, they stepped into the dark, cold entrance. Their flashlights showed the walls and ceiling were lined with large timbers. There was room to walk upright and the tunnel was wide enough to walk side-by-side. The air was damp but the walls were bone dry.

"It's perfect," marveled Ashley. "How could it stay in such good condition for so long?"

Matthew checked the walls carefully. The tunnel was solid rock. "I don't think we need to worry. Only an earthquake could close this shaft."

Ashley relaxed...at least she didn't need to worry about a cave-in.

"Think of the work that went into building this tunnel," said Jonathan. "The miners must have blasted the rock with dynamite and carried all the pieces outside. It must have been hard work. They were dreaming of finding gold. In a way, the mine was built with dreams."

"Dreams build adventures, too," said Ashley. "We're dreaming about Matthew's treasure and that makes us keep going."

"I wonder if the miners found gold?" asked Matthew. "They sure did lots of work for nothing if they didn't."

After walking for several minutes, they sensed something changing. The sound of their footsteps echoed differently.

"Something weird is going on," said Jonathan.

"It's water," whispered Ashley. "I hear water running." The boys were relieved. If Ashley heard water, there was water. She could hear a pin drop across a room.

Ashley pointed her flashlight straight ahead. They moved forward together. Before they knew it, the tunnel walls and ceiling disappeared. They had entered a gigantic cavern. There was enough room in it for ten houses. It was so high their lights barely reached the ceiling. It was huge.

"Over here," said Ashley, excitedly. "There's water running right through the middle...and a pool. It's like a big swimming pool."

"Be careful," warned Jonathan. "There's no telling where that water goes. It must be an underground river."

Ashley leaned over the pool's edge and tested the water with her finger. "Ouch! It's hot. Feel it. It's almost boiling."

The boys dipped their hands in the pool, but pulled back quickly. Matthew's face lit up. "*Warm* water. This is *warm* water!"

They knew there had to be a connection. The secret message said *you must feel flattered and glad.* They had entered the tunnel at Blarney Creek and followed it back toward Gladstone Lakes. Now they found warm water in a hidden cavern. If there was a secret *shipment,* it might be *warm* in the pool they were standing beside.

"I'll bet this river runs out from the mountain behind the cabin we slept in last night," said Jonathan. "If that's true, the secret message makes sense."

"We have to search in the water," said Matthew. "I'm so excited, I'm going to die!"

He stared into the black water and wondered what secrets lay beneath its surface. He was not alone. Ashley and Jonathan were staring, too. The water stared back, like shiny paint on a black sports car.

5

THE LODGE

The new turn of events made them rethink their plans. They agreed to return to the Gladstone Lakes cabin for ropes and other equipment needed to search the pool.

"We should check the rest of the cavern before we go," suggested Ashley.

"I wonder if the grizzly bear from Sekulmun Lake slept here last winter?" asked Matthew.

"Are you trying to ruin this for me?" asked Ashley. "Please stop reminding me of that bear."

They inspected the cavern carefully, using their flashlights to guide them around large boulders that were everywhere. Except for the gentle sound of water, the cavern was silent. Ashley thought how strange it was for them to be alone in a hole in the middle of a Yukon mountain.

Jonathan had friends in California who explored under-ground caves. They called it *spelunking.* They told him of their adventures in a great cave system in Mexico called Sistema Huautla and in the caves under glaciers in Alaska. No one had ever mentioned caves in the Yukon Territory. He wondered if anyone even knew about this cavern.

"Over here," yelled Matthew, as he leaned over a ledge at the far end of the cavern. "There's more water."

Ashley and Jonathan shone their lights below the ledge. There was a small pool of water. The water didn't seem to be moving.

"I'll have a closer look," said Matthew. "Maybe this water is warm, too." He put one foot off the ledge onto the crumbled rock that lay between him and the pool.

"Be careful, Matthew," warned Ashley. "Those rocks don't look safe. Hold my hand so you don't fall."

The three linked hands as Matthew began to slide, inch by inch, toward the water. His feet slipped out from under him, sending a shower of stones into the silent, unmoving pool. "It's like walking on ball bearings. I don't think I can get down."

Jonathan tightened his grip on Ashley's hand as she followed Matthew over the ledge. "You hold Matthew and I'll hold you," he said.

Matthew slid gently toward the water. Jonathan stepped over the ledge. "Just another foot," urged Matthew.

Jonathan climbed down onto the slippery stones,

leaving the safety of the cavern floor. He gripped Ashley's hand tightly. Without warning, Matthew lost his footing and started sliding. In a flash, all three were heading toward the water, hands locked together.

"Stop me!" yelled Matthew. "I can't hold on. I'm falling!" His words were drowned out by Ashley's piercing scream. Noise echoed in the cavern, but no one heard.

As though seeing a slow motion replay, Jonathan watched as Matthew and Ashley were sucked into a strong current lying beneath the calm surface of the pool. He closed his eyes when his turn came. Hitting the water, Jonathan lost his grip on Ashley's hand. His body felt like it had been grabbed by a monster. The underground river immediately smashed him into a wall. For a thin moment he thought it was over. Then the rage continued and his body was swirled around even more.

As suddenly as it started, the violence stopped. Jonathan was barely conscious as he was swept along a stone tube. He wished the water would let him go — his lungs were going to explode.

Ashley was thrown from the water. She wasn't sure if she was alive or dead. She felt pressure on her arm. She tried wiggling her fingers...they still worked. Next, she moved her toes and feet. They felt OK, too. But when she tried to pull herself up, she felt the pressure on her arm again. She pulled, but her arm was stuck. Then she heard a moan.

"Jonathan...Jonathan?" she asked. "Jonathan, is that you?" Ashley was sure it was Jonathan lying on her arm.

"Jonathan...are you all right? Please answer me, Jonathan."

Her twin was slowly regaining awareness. As he tried to focus his mind he thought he could hear someone calling his name again and again. It was a familiar voice, a voice he trusted and loved. He thought he must be on his way to heaven.

"Jonathan, can you hear me? *Please* answer me. Can you move? You're on my arm. I can't move my arm."

"Ashley!" said Jonathan, finding his voice. "Are you all right? Where's Matthew?"

He rolled over and freed Ashley's arm. He began looking for Matthew before realizing he couldn't see in the darkness. He groped around, hoping to find his brother. His hand fell on his backpack, then on a flashlight. He tried the switch. It still worked! "Where's Matthew?" he asked, as if someone would answer.

"I'm over here," came a small voice. "Are you all right?"

Jonathan shone the light in the direction of Matthew's voice. There was only a wall of rock. Then Matthew appeared out of nowhere. The twins were startled.

"Are you guys OK?" asked Matthew. "Ashley, you're a wreck!"

"Thanks, Matthew. Have you checked a mirror lately?"

Each had a few scrapes and sore spots, but no injuries appeared serious. Ashley and Matthew still had their backpacks on. They wondered if the packs hadn't saved their lives when they were pounded into the walls.

They were in a narrow tunnel. The underground river

entered at one end and made a sharp turn. They had been thrown clear of the water at the turn. At the other end the river disappeared into the wall of the mountain again. There was no way out!

Matthew found a crack in the wall. It was large enough to squeeze through if they removed their packs. Once again they found themselves in a cavern. This one was much smaller than the one they had left just a short time before.

After their experience in the water, they thought nothing could surprise them. Then they heard voices.

"There's someone else here," whispered Ashley.

Jonathan's first thought was to find the voices and get help. But his intuition told him to be careful. "Wait," he whispered, "remember last night? Whoever is here might not be happy to see us."

The voices didn't come closer, so they crept across the cavern, keeping their flashlights covered. Soon they heard the voices clearly and saw the glow of light made by a single bulb at the far end of the cave. Two men talked loudly.

"It woulda' been somethin' to see. Them kids were probably scared out of their skulls. When the girl screamed after I busted the window, my eardrums near broke. Brats. Can't figure out what they were doin' up here by themselves, know what I mean? They're just kids."

"I don't know why they were pokin' around, but I'm glad Eloise mentioned them. We can't afford havin' some kids mess up our operation. It'd be just our luck for three dumb kids to louse up the whole deal."

"Quit worrying, they're long gone. This morning I saw them taking the trail to Sekulmun Lake. That's probably where they came from in the first place. They won't be back."

Ashley, Jonathan and Matthew couldn't believe what they were hearing. The man who broke their window the night before was standing only twenty feet away. These men weren't going to help them to get out of the cave.

The men were working at a large table. It was impossible to see what they were doing. On the floor lay numerous crates, some open, others closed. There were piles of equipment lying around; ropes, small pulleys, metal pins and gadgets they didn't recognize. On the table they saw rolls of heavy brown wrapping paper, piles of plastic bags and weigh scales with bright red digital numbers.

Jonathan pointed to a wall beside the table. It was lined with a dozen rifles and shotguns. Boxes of ammunition were stacked nearby. Whatever was going on here must be serious business, he thought.

"We've been at this long enough," said the bigger of the two men, the one who had attacked their cabin. "I'm takin' a break."

"Sure, let's take a break," responded his partner. "They have the motorhome set up, so we gotta have this stuff ready by tonight. Marty's comin' up later today...we'll send this stuff out with him when he flies back." The two men moved off into what must have been another tunnel. A heavy door slammed.

Ashley spoke first. "What's going on? Did you see those two creeps?"

"Creeps?" asked Jonathan. "Ash, those guys are heavy-jumbo thugs. Look at the guns. They could start a small war."

"What were they doing?" asked Matthew. "They left the light on. Let's have a look." He stepped from their hiding place and walked toward the table.

"Matthew," whispered Ashley, "don't touch anything."

The crates were full of mountain climbing equipment, most of it new. They found torches used for welding metal. The bags the men had been packing and weighing were filled with a white powder.

"Jonathan," said Ashley, nervously, "I think these bags are filled with drugs."

Jonathan examined the bags. "Maybe it's heroin."

"Not the kind of treasure I had in mind," muttered Matthew. "Now we're stuck in a hole with nothing but drug smugglers between us and the police. What a bummer."

"We have to tell the police what's going on," said Ashley. "How are we going to get out?"

"We have no choice but to follow those men," said Jonathan.

"They'll see us for sure, Jonathan," said Matthew.

"We have no choice," repeated Jonathan. "We can't get out the way we came in."

"True," agreed Ashley. "Let's see where they went."

They entered the tunnel where the two men had

disappeared. There they found stairs leading to the cave's roof. At the top of the stairs was a heavy trap door.

"Maybe it opens outside somewhere and they won't see us," said Matthew.

"Or maybe it opens into their living room," countered Ashley.

Jonathan tried to think how they could escape. "Here's what we'll do. We'll climb to the top and try the door. If it opens, you go through first, Matthew. Ashley, you go next. If it looks like trouble, run in different directions. One of us might get away and be able to contact the police."

They climbed the stairs. Jonathan pushed the door...it lifted silently. Through the narrow crack he could see only darkness. He eased the door ajar until there was room for Matthew to climb out.

Matthew crawled through the opening. He couldn't see anything as he held the door open for the twins.

"At least we're out of the cave," whispered Jonathan.

"Yes," said Ashley, "but what have we gotten ourselves into?"

6

FRYING PAN TO FIRE

"There's no one here," said Matthew. They turned on their flashlights...they were in a space between two walls. Jonathan guessed it was four feet wide and six feet long.

"Nothing," said Matthew. "Just four bare walls."

Ashley felt uncomfortable. She didn't like small, confining spaces. Her heart beat faster. "This is stupid."

"It's weird," said Matthew. "How did those men get out?"

"That's right...there has to be a way out." Ashley felt better knowing there had to be a solution.

"There must be a hidden door or secret panel," said Jonathan. "All we have to do is find it."

"Here it is," said Matthew, almost instantly. He seemed to have an ability to find hidden things. He pointed to a small button in the wall. Jonathan and Ashley could only tell it was there by touching it.

"Let's push it and see what happens," suggested Matthew.

"Matthew," said Ashley, "don't push the button until we know what we're going to do."

"Simple," said Matthew, "we push it and run as fast as we can. Right, Jonathan?"

"I think he's right, Ash. That's all we can do."

"All right, Matthew," she said, "push the button and get ready to run."

Matthew pushed the button and the wall moved. There was no sound as it slid away.

A luxurious office with leather furniture and Oriental carpets appeared before them. Across the room was a desk and a doorway. At the desk sat a small man with a thin face. He saw them at the same instant they saw him. His beady eyes grew large with surprise. As they raced through the office door, he was shouting: "Stop those kids. Someone stop those kids."

Beyond the door was a stairway. They flew down the stairs two at a time. Behind them the little man recovered from his surprise and roared. "Someone better stop those damn kids!"

The plan is working, thought Ashley.

At the bottom of the stairs were sliding glass doors leading to a large deck. Jonathan led the way, barely catching a glimpse of the two men from the cavern barging down the stairs after them.

From the deck to the ground took only an instant. They

ran for the trees, running faster than they knew they could. The fear of being caught provided extra energy. Behind them the big man tripped on a tree root and fell head over heels, cursing loudly.

After running for several minutes they came to the edge of the lake. Ducking back into the trees and following the shore, they left the Lodge farther and farther behind.

Matthew ran out of gas first. "I'm bushed," he said, panting for breath. "I need a rest...can't run any more... need to sit down..." He sprawled to the ground.

Ashley and Jonathan joined him. Their legs felt like rubber.

THE FLIGHT

Exhausted, they listened for their pursuers.

"I don't hear anything," said Ashley. She recovered faster than the boys. "I'm going to see if those men are coming along the shore. You two stay here."

"Be careful," warned Jonathan. "Those dopeheads are seriously mad at us. If they catch us, we're finished."

Walking cautiously, Ashley wondered if she and her brothers had done the right thing. Of course, they didn't know they'd fall into an underground river. It wasn't their fault they had to run for their lives to escape from the Lodge. Still, she felt responsible for the fix they were in. What would her father think?

Her thoughts wandered. She thought about her friend Ben. Jonathan teased her, saying Ben was her boyfriend,

45

but it wasn't true. Still, she liked him. It would be fun if he could be here in the Yukon with them.

At the shore, Ashley listened carefully. She heard voices in the distance, but they drifted in and out on the breeze. She couldn't see anyone along the edge of the lake.

"See anything?"

Ashley jumped at the unexpected sound. "Jonathan Adams! Don't you have any brains? You're as bad as Matthew the way you creep around."

"Sorry," said Jonathan.

"Sorry? Why can't you guys plug into what's going on around you? What is it with boys that makes them so dense, anyway?" She was tired of the way her brothers and other boys seemed unaware of other people's feelings. It seemed as if boys didn't know how to pay attention to anything but themselves.

"I said I'm sorry." He knew Ashley was tired. He also knew she was right. Because they were twins, they did many things the same way. But Ashley was always more in tune with her surroundings than he was.

"I hear something," said Matthew. "Hear it?" he asked, pointing across the lake.

"I can't hear anything," said Jonathan.

"It's a plane," said Ashley.

A dot appeared over the south end of the lake. The engine's drone became louder as the plane descended toward the water. They retreated to the trees.

The pilot swooped low, circling the lake to make sure it

was safe to land. Jonathan made his usual identification. "Cessna 206, useful payload..."

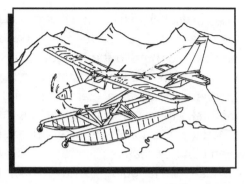

"It's heading for the Lodge," said Matthew. "Let's go closer so we can spy on them."

"We've had enough excitement for one day, Matthew," said Ashley. "We're not spying on anything."

"She's right, Matt," said Jonathan. "Besides, we just ran away from those people. It wouldn't make sense to press our luck."

"I just want to see what they're doing. Don't you want to know what they're up to?"

"No," replied Ashley and Jonathan simultaneously.

Matthew wasn't convinced. "Can we just move where we can watch the plane? We can stay out of sight and just sort of watch with the binoculars, know what I mean?"

Jonathan shrugged.

"Please, Ash," begged Matthew. "We're safe now... they're not even chasing us. It's getting late, so we can't go anywhere tonight. It won't hurt to watch."

Ashley gave in. "OK, OK. We'll go where we can see the plane. But that's all we do...just watch the plane."

"All right!" whooped Matthew.

The plane pulled up to the dock in front of the Lodge.

They saw the two men who had chased them shake hands with the pilot. The men then unloaded several large crates and carried them to the Lodge.

"Those are the kind of crates we saw in the cave," said Matthew. "They take them there and do something and then take them somewhere else on the plane."

Ashley and Jonathan were less interested in the crates than Matthew was.

"Matt, we're going to have to dry our clothes," said Jonathan.

"Mine aren't that wet," replied Matthew, keeping an eye on the plane.

"Mine are and I'm getting cold," said Jonathan. "We should start a fire and dry out."

Ashley was cold, too. She didn't want to light a fire, afraid someone from the Lodge might see the smoke. But she knew they had to get warm, especially if they were going to camp for the night. "C'mon, Jonathan. We'll build a fire and Matthew can keep his eye on the plane."

"Cool," said Matthew, still watching the plane.

Jonathan and Ashley retreated to the cover of the trees.

"Look at him staring at the plane," Jonathan said. "He won't take his eyes off it. It's like he's zoned out, but he isn't. He loves searching for things, doesn't he?"

Ashley smiled as she gathered twigs for a fire. "For sure. He gets something in his head and stays with it until he's satisfied. Like Dad says, he's persistent."

"You're persistent, too, and so am I. But Matthew's not just persistent, Ash. It's something else. The things that interest him are things other people think are boring. He doesn't care what others think and then he makes those ordinary things interesting. I don't know how he does it."

Ashley agreed. "Dad says Matthew sees potential where other people don't see anything at all. Because he sees possibilities, he looks harder. That's what he does, like you said...he looks for things."

They heard an engine roar to life.

"Hey Matthew," shouted Jonathan, "is the plane taking off already?" There was no reply as the roar of the motor grew louder.

"Matthew," called Ashley, "what's going on?"

Matthew didn't reply. Jonathan and Ashley ran to the edge of the trees. Matthew was gone. On the lake the plane was circling. Its engine whined as it prepared for takeoff.

The plane gathered speed and its floats rose in the water. It was coming toward Ashley and Jonathan. They crouched behind a rock as it lifted off. The pilot threw the plane's nose sharply into the air and zoomed overhead.

It was a good thing they kept their eyes on the plane. From a rear window Matthew's face stared back at them. In his eyes they saw a pleading look. Matthew was in trouble again.

7

SILVER CITY

Matthew decided to risk being seen by the pilot. He rose to the window as the plane bounced and shook like a leaf in a windstorm. He saw Ashley and Jonathan on shore and hoped they saw him.

He dropped to the floor. For the first time in his life he was glad he was small. The pilot couldn't see him crouched behind a seat near the back of the plane. His heart pounded as fast as it had when he was running from the Lodge. He thought the pilot would hear it. He wondered how his heart could be going so fast when he wasn't even moving.

Not my most excellent move, he told himself. If Ashley and Jonathan save me this time, I'll never hassle them again. Never! He closed his eyes and prayed the pilot wouldn't find him or, if he did, at least wouldn't kill him. He couldn't see how to get out of this situation. He felt embarrassed. His father would disown him and probably never take him on a vacation again. He wished he could disappear.

He hadn't meant this to happen. He'd slipped down to the plane for a closer look when no one was around. The next thing he knew the pilot jumped in and started the engine.

As he worried about his ruined reputation, Matthew saw a set of headphones lying on the floor. He put them on and heard voices.

"Silver City, Silver City. This is CFN 152. Do you copy? Over."

"CFN 152, this is Silver City. How ya doin', Marty? Over."

"Perfect, dude. I'm headin' in from Happyrock. Be about ten minutes. Cultus Bay is just ahead. Over."

"No problem, Marty. Everything's cool here. See anything unusual? Over."

"Negative. Looks like Fast Freddy's cookin' hot dogs, hamburgers and french fries. There's more smoke comin' out of his place than if it was on fire. Over."

"I'm not surprised. He lost his wife for a week. She's in Whitehorse Hospital getting tests. He's working the claim with his boy. Over."

"His boy? I never knew Fast Freddy had a son. Over."

"That's a big ten-four. His boy is seventy-two next week. Gotta go. Over and out."

The pilot laughed aloud. Matthew was relieved to learn

their destination was close to Gladstone Lakes. A fifteen minute plane ride couldn't take them very far away.

Minutes later the plane banked sharply and began losing altitude. Through the windows Matthew saw a panorama of dark, jagged snow-capped mountains. The mountains gave way to an expanse of pink sky — sunset on Kluane Lake.

At the bottom of the turn they dropped quickly, straightened out and bounced onto a rough landing strip. Matthew had expected to land on water but now he realized the plane had wheels *and* floats. The pilot taxied to a small building, grabbed his pack from behind his seat and jumped to the ground.

The echo of the plane's engine soon faded from Matthew's ears, leaving silence. Though the sky was pink, the sun had set and the summer darkness shrouded Kluane Lake. Matthew shivered in the cold night air.

I have to get out of here, he thought. But where could he go? Now that he was alone, he wasn't having fun. At home he often wanted to be left alone but right now he would give his roller blades to see Ashley or Jonathan.

Climbing from the plane, he wondered what kind of city Silver City was. There seemed to be only one building. He heard the *whoosh* of a distant car. He heard it again. There's a road nearby, he thought. I have to get to that road.

The building turned out to be a trailer. The front door was open and the doorway filled with light. Matthew listened.

52

"All I know is we gotta tell the boss there's trouble."

"I know, Marty. It's just...I mean...what the hell's the big deal? So what if a couple of kids nosed around the Lodge? What harm can a couple of kids do? Once they see that big German, Gurder, they'll be scared to death. It's small time."

"They're worried, man. They're packin' the stuff out tonight and stashin' it across the lake. Remember, if they get busted, we get busted. I ain't in no mood for prison. Just be careful." Marty paused to let the message sink in.

"They told me to leave a message for the boss at the bar in Haines Junction tomorrow."

"Whatever you say, Marty. Except there are two people to take up to Happyrock first thing in the morning. Hikers from New Yawk City. You never heard such loud people. They'll be there for four days, so we'll have time to work on their motorhome. It's one of them bus jobs — big sucker."

"I'll take 'em up first, then fly to the Junction. Any coffee in the pot?"

As the men shuffled about the trailer, Matthew decided to find the road. He followed the sound of the moving cars. Soon he discovered it wasn't going to be as easy as he thought. His flashlight was almost dead and it cast only enough light to make every rock look like a bear or a wolf. The shadows were scary.

It was also difficult to keep his footing. Stones the size of footballs were everywhere. The large gravel was polished smooth and he had to pick his way carefully.

After half an hour of slow progress, he listened again for passing cars. *Whoosh. Whoosh.* The sounds were no closer than when he started. He 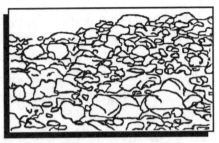 became frightened. He stood alone in the Yukon, not knowing what to do next. Tears filled his eyes.

Then he heard his worst nightmare.

Whap...whap...whap....whap. It was a steady sound — and it was coming closer.

Whap...whap...whap...whap.

Matthew froze. "I'm history," he thought, frantically. Suddenly, the sound stopped not ten feet from him.

"What you say?" came a strange voice. "What's that you say? Is someone hiding? Speak up, whoever you are."

"It...it's just me," managed Matthew.

"Eh?" The woman came closer. "Why are you saying you are history?" she asked.

"I...I didn't say anything," said Matthew. He could barely speak.

"Yes, you did, young man. I heard you with my own two ears. But it doesn't matter...who cares about that?" She leaned forward. "Tell me what you are doing here alone so late at night? Are you lost?"

"Yes, I'm lost...I guess. My name is Matthew Adams and I'm in big trouble. Would you help me?"

She smiled. "Of course I will help you, Matthew Adams.

My name is Helga. Come with me." She led Matthew to the path she had been running on. "So, Matthew, what kind of trouble are you in?"

"It's a long story," he said. "Why are you out here at night?"

"Me? I am jogging so I do not get too much weight on my hips. At night it is quiet and cool...a good time to run. And you? Were you jogging?" She laughed cheerfully at her little joke.

"Where do you live?" asked Matthew.

"I live where we are going...in my trailer. You will see. I conduct research here at Kluane Lake for my University in Germany. I am a climatologist."

"A what? What's a climatologist?"

"I study the climate...you know, the weather."

They soon arrived at a trailer in the middle of nowhere. There were several trailers together. Helga explained this was an environmental research station where people studied weather patterns and environmental changes like acid rain and airborne pollution.

"You put on these dry clothes and tell me about the trouble you are in. We can have a sandwich if you're hungry. Are you hungry?"

"Starved," said Matthew. He liked her. She was nice, and pretty, too. He wished his father would marry someone like Helga.

Matthew told her how he, Ashley and Jonathan found a cave under the Lodge at Gladstone Lakes and how they were chased into the woods. He also told her he had been investigating the plane when the pilot, Marty, took off with him on board.

"That's an exciting story. But I don't think those men wanted to hurt you," she said.

"Maybe...but I think they're hiding something in the cave. There were guns and ammunition. How many Lodges have a secret sliding wall leading to an underground cave?" He felt better now that he had told an adult about the cave.

"I'll tell you what we'll do," she said. "In the morning, after we both get some sleep, we'll call the R.C.M.P. and tell them what happened. They will get you back to your brother and sister at Gladstone Lakes. How does that sound?"

Matthew agreed. "The R.C.M.P....is that the Royal Canadian Mounted Police? Do they have horses?"

Helga laughed as she led him to a bunk at the rear of the trailer. "I'm afraid not, Matthew. Here in the Yukon they have cars, trucks, boats, snowmobiles, dogsleds, and airplanes — but no horses. In the morning you can ask Corporal Swanson all the questions you like. For now, you must get some sleep. You're much too young to miss your sleep."

Helga smiled once more as she tucked the small boy in. He was asleep before she walked away.

8

THE REUNION

"Hello, son," said the handsome policeman. He held his hand out to Matthew. "My name is Corporal Swanson of the Royal Canadian Mounted Police."

Matthew was thrilled. He'd finished eating a big breakfast when Corporal Swanson arrived. "Hello, sir. Where's your uniform? Don't you wear a righteous red suit?"

Swanson laughed. "Son, I don't wear my uniform in the bush. Just my jeans, like everyone else. What's this I hear about you stowing away on Marty's aircraft?"

"I didn't really stow away, sir. I was sort of kidnaped."

"Kidnaped, were you? That's a serious crime."

"Not really kidnaped. It was more like an accident, I guess."

"What were you doing on Marty's plane, son?" Corporal

Swanson had a more serious look on his face now.

"Well, like I told Helga, we were suspicious about what was going on, you know, at the Lodge."

"Yes, Helga told me. How did you get in the cave under the Lodge in the first place?"

Matthew told the officer how he and the twins fell into the underground river and then found themselves in the cavern under the Lodge. Matthew didn't say anything about the treasure. He knew the story was strange enough without mentioning the secret message.

"That's quite a story. I've never heard of any caves around Gladstone." He turned to Helga. "Thanks for looking after the boy. Marty's flying up to the Lodge this morning. I'll take Matthew and we'll find his brother and sister. Then we'll go to the Lodge and see if there's anything funny going on."

"Great," exclaimed Matthew. "You could come, too, Helga. Could Helga come with us, sir?"

Helga laughed. A laugh never seemed far from her pretty face.

"You men can go and play, Matthew. For myself, I have plenty of work right here." She ruffled Matthew's hair playfully. "Remember to get a ticket before you get in an airplane in the future."

On their way to the airstrip Matthew could see where he had walked the night before — there were no bears or wolves.

"Tell me, Matt," said Swanson, "what are you and your family doing at Gladstone Lakes? Are your parents hiking into the high country?"

"We're visiting Sekulmun Lake," replied Matthew. "We hiked to Gladstone Lakes for fun. We didn't know there would be other people there."

"Sekulmun Lake? Hmmm...how far away is that?"

"Not far. It didn't take us long to walk from Sekulmun to Gladstone. About a day and a half. Could I ask you a question, sir?"

"Shoot."

"Where is Silver City?"

"Silver City? Right beside the airstrip. It's not a city, not now. It was a rest stop during gold rush days. Now there are only abandoned log cabins. It's a ghost town. What do you think of Kluane Lake?" He waved his arm toward the lake that seemed to go on forever.

"I like it here," said Matthew. "I wish Jonathan and Ashley could see it."

"There's Marty, loading the plane. Looks like he has passengers. Hey, Marty, do you have room for two more?"

"Sure do, Corporal Swanson. Who's your friend?"

"Marty, I'd like you to meet Matthew Adams. We have some business at Gladstone. We'd appreciate a ride."

"Climb aboard. We'll be leavin' in five minutes."

Soon they were flying over the most rugged wilderness on earth. Marty said the mountains were part of the Ruby Range. Much of the Yukon's gold had come from here during the gold rush. "Gold nuggets bigger than your hand come out of those mountains, even today."

Matthew looked below. He saw something move.

"What's that?"

"Dall sheep," said Marty. "Lambs and ewes. The rams are off by themselves for the summer. I'd say there are thirty or more in that group."

Before Matthew realized it, the plane descended toward a pair of dark blue lakes. Gladstone Lakes were really in high country, he thought. They circled and landed smoothly on the water. He watched through the window for Ashley and Jonathan, but they were nowhere to be seen.

The two men who had chased him yesterday were at the dock to greet the passengers. They recognized Corporal Swanson. Marty introduced them to Matthew.

The big man's name was Gurder and his partner was Leo. Leo looked like an outdoorsman but Gurder belonged in a Los Angeles health spa.

"Have you gentlemen seen a teenage girl and boy?" asked Swanson. "They're Matthew's brother and sister."

"No sir," replied Leo. "Haven't seen anyone except our guests."

"All right. We'll have to find them and then we'll drop into the Lodge for a visit. Tell Harry to expect us."

Corporal Swanson and Matthew began their search.

"Ashley...Jonathan, it's me," shouted Matthew. "I'm OK. I'm here with Corporal Swanson of the Mounted Police. He's going to help us. Are you there?"

There was no response. Matthew went to the spot where Ashley and Jonathan had their campfire. "They were right here. I thought they would wait for me. I was sure they would wait."

From high above he heard a familiar voice.

"We did wait, Matthew Adams. Not that I know why."

Matthew looked up. Sure enough, Ashley and Jonathan were hiding in a tree. They smiled — and Matthew smiled, too.

RETURN TO THE LODGE

Matthew knew Jonathan and Ashley were impressed he had brought a policeman back with him. He knew he would have to explain why he had been in the plane in the first place, but they would agree he had accomplished something.

"We're going to go to the Lodge and look at your cavern," said Swanson. "If Harry is doing something illegal, we'll find out."

"Don't you need a search warrant?" asked Ashley.

Swanson laughed. "This is the Yukon Territory, Ashley. If Harry won't let me look around, I'll know something is wrong. We won't need a warrant."

"I can't wait for you to see the cave, sir," said Jonathan. "There's a humidifier, lights, welding equipment...and electronic scales, guns, ammunition. It's a lot of stuff."

At the Lodge the first person they met was Eloise.

"*Hi,* kids. Where did you find *this* handsome specimen? Are you their *father?*"

Something about Eloise triggered a weird part of Matthew's personality. "No, Eloise, he's not our father. He's Corporal Swanson of the Mounted Police."

"A *Mountie!*" gushed Eloise. "How exciting! We Americans think very highly of the Canadian Mounties. I feel so much safer now that you're here. It's too bad I'm leaving tomorrow. I'd love you to show me around your forest."

Matthew rolled his eyes impatiently.

"Tell me," continued Eloise, edging closer to the policeman, "have you ever wrestled with a grizzly bear, Officer Swanson?"

"Eloise," said Matthew, "Corporal Swanson has work to do. He doesn't want to wrestle with you."

Neither Eloise nor Swanson were paying attention to Matthew. The Mountie was gazing into Eloise's eyes and it was obvious he'd like to wrestle with her.

"Uhh, pleased to meet you, ma'am," muttered Swanson. "The little guy is right...we have to go...official business. Maybe later, if you'd like, I could take you fishing."

"Fishing?" asked Eloise, flashing her nicest smile. "I'd *love* to. Imagine...fishing with a Canadian Mountie! Tell you what. I'll wait here on the deck while you finish whatever you're doing with my friends. Then we'll go fishing."

Matthew was totally disgusted. He led the others through the door, almost bumping into Harry, the little man who had been sitting at the desk when they came through the sliding wall.

"Corporal Swanson," said Harry, "it's a pleasure to see you. Can I get you coffee? Kids, would you like a soda?"

"No thanks, Harry," said Swanson. "Harry, I met young Matthew over at Silver City. Helga, a researcher at the Kluane Lake station, found him wandering around last night. To make a long story short, Matthew, Jonathan and Ashley say there's a cavern under the Lodge and Leo and Gurder were there yesterday. They say there's a sliding wall leading from the cavern to your office. I thought I should check it out."

Ashley watched Harry closely. He seemed genuinely surprised.

"A secret wall?" he asked. "A cavern under the Lodge? You're joking, of course."

"No, we're not joking," said Jonathan.

"Kids," said Harry, "don't you realize you can get in trouble telling wild stories?"

"There *is* a cavern under the Lodge," insisted Matthew. "We were in it yesterday."

"Corporal, I don't know what they're talking about. The Lodge has only been open for two years, as you know. If there was a secret passage, I would know about it."

Harry continued. "We don't want negative stories floating around about the Lodge. We have a lot of money invested here and we're just getting established. If there's anything I can do to clear this up, I'm prepared to do it."

Corporal Swanson hesitated a moment, then turned to Jonathan. "I guess that's it. What do you think, kids? Are you satisfied?"

"Satisfied?" asked Ashley. "Satisfied with what? We haven't done anything."

"Miss," said Harry, his voice calm, "do you think a crime has been committed?"

Ashley understood. Of course, no crime had been committed. "May we go to your office and look for the sliding door?" she asked. "Right now?"

"Certainly," said Harry. "But let's make a deal. You look as long as you like. If you don't find what you're looking for, you promise to stop telling your silly story. We don't need negative publicity. Deal?"

"OK," said Matthew, "it's a deal. Let's go." He started up the stairs. At the top of the stairs were three doors. They knew it wasn't the first door. But which of the other two? They weren't sure.

Harry opened one of the doors. "In here?"

They looked in the room. Nothing looked familiar. "Must be the next one," said Ashley. Harry led them to the next room.

"This is it," stated Matthew. "This is the room. The wall is over there."

"Is this it?" Swanson asked Jonathan.

"Yes, sir, this is the room. I remember it. Right, Ash?" She nodded.

Jonathan and Ashley joined Matthew at the sliding wall. They searched for a separation in the wall, but couldn't find anything. No matter how hard they looked, the wall looked normal in every respect.

Corporal Swanson pounded the wall with his hand. "Sounds solid." He went around the room searching for a false wall.

Matthew was frantic. He'd found the secret button on the other side of the wall, so why couldn't he figure out this side? "What's going on?" he whispered to Jonathan. "Why can't we find it? Corporal Swanson's going to think I lied."

"Something's fishy, we know that. We just can't prove it, I guess."

Harry and Swanson stood in the doorway discussing the situation. "It looks like Harry's right, kids," said the police officer. "He's agreed not to press charges for trespassing on the plane yesterday. But you have to agree to stop interfering with the Lodge. Is it a deal?"

"Corporal Swanson," said Matthew, "I wasn't lying about the wall." He was almost in tears. "Honest, I wasn't."

The Mountie placed his arm around Matthew's shoulder as they went down the stairs. "I know, son. I can see you're trustworthy. I'm going to keep an eye on the Lodge. If we find any illegal activities, I'll personally let you know. How's that?"

Matthew's faith was restored in a flash. "It's a deal, sir," he said.

Once outside, on the deck, Swanson spoke to Ashley and Jonathan. "Will you be all right going back to the lake? What was the name of the lake?"

"Sekulmun," replied Ashley.

"Right, Sekulmun. Will you be able to get there by

yourselves? Do you have enough food?"

Ashley assured him they would be fine. Since it was still early morning and the trip was downhill, Jonathan thought they might make it to Sekulmun that same day.

"I'm sorry things turned out this way," said Swanson. "But don't worry, we'll take care of everything."

Eloise joined them. "Are you kids leaving? Be careful. Watch out for bears. Matthew, take care of your sister. She shouldn't be out in the wild forest with you boys."

Ashley groaned inwardly. As they left the Lodge, she was sad their adventure had ended this way. She decided the only thing they could do was leave it in the hands of the authorities.

9

RETURN TO SEKULMUN

T he return hike to Sekulmun Lake was easy.
Though they wanted to search for the treasure,
they knew their father might have returned by now.
If so, he would be worried. They also realized their
father's help would be needed if they were to find the
hidden shipment. They had worn out their welcome at the
Lodge — showing up again would probably land them in
trouble. The best thing was to go straight back to
Sekulmun.

Their father was not at the cabin. The note they had left
telling him about their hike to Gladstone Lakes was still on
the table.

"Outstanding!" said Matthew. "I was sure Dad would be
here and be mad at us. At least everything didn't turn out
to be a bummer today." He collapsed on his bunk. "I've

never been so tired in my life."

They were all tired. Jonathan made sandwiches while Ashley sat at the table with the secret message. She was trying to put the events of the past few days together in her mind. It was like trying to put pieces of a puzzle together. The problem was that she wasn't sure if the pieces belonged to the same puzzle.

"Do you think there's real treasure in the cave?" she asked Jonathan.

"Something's there. The clues point to it. Maybe there's nothing now, but I'll bet there was once." He glanced at Matthew's bunk. "Look at him. He's sound asleep."

"I hope Dad thinks it's worth looking for," said Ashley. "Matthew's heart would be broken if we didn't try."

"Can you imagine how scared he was when that plane took off with him in it? What a shock it must have been. Even if we don't find any treasure, we had a good time."

Ashley and Jonathan ate their sandwiches and settled into their bunks. In the world's big cities cars roared along freeways, but in the Yukon there was only silence. It was as though there was only a limited amount of noise and hurry available in the world. Since other places used it all up, the Yukon was left with none. That's what it seemed like at Sekulmun Lake.

THE VISITOR

Morning brought another day of blue skies and bright sunshine — the kind of morning that lures thousands of visitors to the North every year.

"Wake up. Wake up, you guys." Matthew was very excited. "Wake up. There's an airplane coming. Hurry. It's going to land...I think it's Dad!" Satisfied they were awake, Matthew flew out the door. He watched the plane drone its way toward him. Moments later it circled low and headed in for a landing.

"Is it Dad?" asked Ashley.

"Cessna 180," said Jonathan. "Cruise speed about 150 m.p.h. at 7500 feet, 225 horsepower Continental engine, seats four, loads maybe a thousand or more pounds. Great bush plane. There's only one person in the plane, Matthew, and it isn't Dad."

Jonathan was right. Their father wasn't in the plane. They could see the pilot's face as he guided the plane across the lake's smooth surface. The pilot nudged the floats 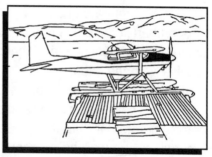 against the dock, hopped out and secured the plane.

"Hi, kids," he said, waving. "Great day, eh?"

"Hello," said Jonathan.

The pilot was average height with dark brown skin that looked like leather. He looked both young and old. The most noticeable thing about him, however, was his police uniform.

"Can a man get a cup of coffee around here?" he asked

with a grin, looking at Ashley.

"Sure," said Jonathan. "Come on back to the cabin and I'll make some." Jonathan introduced himself and the others.

"Glad to meet you. My name is Johnny Johnson. Constable Johnny Johnson, Royal Canadian Mounted Police. You can call me Johnny. Good to see you arrived safely from Gladstone Lakes. Have any trouble on the trail?"

"No, sir," said Matthew. He was staring at the visitor.

"I've heard a lot about you, Matthew. I'm told you make quite an impression on people. So you had no problems getting back yesterday, eh?"

"No, sir," repeated Matthew, continuing to stare.

Jonathan lit the stove and put on a pot of water. Seated at the table, Constable Johnson looked like he was familiar with the cabin.

"Done any fishing here at Sekulmun?" he asked.

"A bit," said Ashley. "We didn't have much chance before our father had to go back to California for an emergency. He warned us about the wind on the lake, so we haven't gone out."

"There are big fish in this lake," continued the Constable. "When I was a kid, we caught a fifty-two-pound trout here. Across the lake, maybe five miles down. That's one big trout, let me tell you. Damn near swamped the boat. That fish weighed more than I did at the time. Do you have Pixees?"

"What's a Pixee?" asked Ashley.

70

"A lure. Real effective in the Yukon. Good in Alaska, too."

"Are you Canadian?" asked Matthew.

"Matthew!" said Ashley, embarrassed.

The police officer smiled. He was aware of Matthew's open curiosity. "Yes, son, I'm a Canadian. In fact, I'm sort of an original Canadian. I'm Indian. Tutchone. My people lived in these mountains before there was a Sekulmun Lake...or a Canada, for that matter. Centuries ago, when your ancestors lived in Europe, my ancestors followed the caribou and admired the grizzly bear right here."

"If you're a policeman, you must have a badge, right? Like the F.B.I.? May I see your badge?"

"Matthew," said Ashley. "What's with you? You acted the same way with Eloise. It isn't funny."

This jarred Matthew from his own little world. "I'm sorry, Ash. I just asked a question."

"Here you go," said Johnny, taking his identification from his jacket. "He's right, Ashley. I should have shown my ID." He placed it in front of Matthew.

Matthew's eyes widened. He touched the large silver badge. Around the rim were the words *Royal Canadian Mounted Police*. He looked at Johnny Johnson with new respect. "Why didn't Corporal Swanson have a uniform?" he asked.

"Sekulmun Lake," exclaimed Ashley. "He didn't know where Sekulmun Lake was!"

The others looked at her. Something Swanson said had been bothering Ashley since they left Gladstone Lakes.

She only now figured it out.

"Corporal Swanson didn't know where Sekulmun Lake was," she repeated. "Any Yukon police officer should know that, right?"

"You're right," agreed Matthew. "He asked me the same thing at Silver City."

"Corporal Swanson?" asked Johnny.

They told him about the cavern, Matthew's flight to Silver City, Helga, and Corporal Swanson. Johnny listened with increasing interest.

"Ms. Hodge didn't have to worry about you three," he said when they finished. "You can take care of your-selves."

"Ms. Hodge?" asked Jonathan and Ashley. Everyone stopped talking. Everyone had questions. The cabin fell silent.

"Ms. Hodge — the lady who suggested we check to make sure you were all right. Early this morning she reported you were hiking to Sekulmun Lake from Glad-stone Lakes. She filed the report at the Haines Junction detachment. She knows you," continued Johnny, "because she said she was going to ask Matthew for a date when he's older."

"Eloise!" said Matthew, blushing. "Ms. Hodge is Eloise."

"That's right. She picked up her

motorhome in Silver City and filed the report in the Junction. She's driving home to New York."

"Now we know who Ms. Hodge is," said Ashley. "Do you know Corporal Swanson?"

"Of the Mounted Police?" asked Matthew.

"There's no Corporal Swanson in the Mounted Police," said Johnny. He was very sure of himself.

"He didn't wear a uniform," said Matthew.

"We wear a uniform on duty. Did he show you his ID, Matthew?"

"No, sir, he didn't."

"Impersonating a police officer is a serious crime. There must be a reason for deceiving you. Start at the beginning and tell me everything. Don't leave out any details."

They told their story, happy to have found someone who wanted to hear it. Johnny listened carefully, asking questions and taking notes.

"Things happen when you kids are around, eh? My grandfather talked about caves in those mountains and about treasure, too. He said it had something to do with World War II, but we never paid attention." He paused, as though reflecting for a moment on an old memory.

"As for the Lodge...they must be up to something. If I arrest whoever this Swanson is, they'll stop what they're doing and we may never find out what's going on. I'll have to think about this over another cup of coffee."

"When I heard the men talking in the trailer at Silver City," said Matthew, "they said they were moving the stuff across the lake. Maybe we could find it and you would have enough evidence to arrest them."

"That's right," said Jonathan and Ashley. They sounded like stereo people — they spoke on two channels at the same time.

"We heard them that night," said Jonathan. "They loaded a boat and went across the lake twice. We couldn't see, but we heard them."

"Matthew," said Johnny, "I like your idea. How would you like to go for a ride in my plane? We can investigate the far side of the lake. If they've hidden something, we can find it."

"Rad," said Matthew. "A most excellent idea."

Their interest high once more, they organized their packs and left a new note for their father. As they climbed aboard the plane, Matthew could barely contain his excitement.

"Let's show Mr. Harry we're on to him...and then let's find my treasure!"

10

THE CACHE

The plane sped across the water and lifted into the air. Johnny Johnson flew as easily as others drive a car. In no time they were approaching Gladstone Lakes. Johnny said he would land on the first lake so they couldn't be seen from the Lodge. Ashley tightened her grip as the plane skimmed above tree tops toward the lake. She was certain they would crash in the trees.

They landed on the water with a sharp bump and slowed quickly. Johnny had obviously done this often. He steered toward shore.

"Look!" said Matthew. "An animal...what is it?"

"A big old bull moose," said Johnny. "You have a good eye, Matthew. Maybe you'll come hunting with me, eh?"

"Outstanding," said Matthew. "Did you see him, Ash? How can an animal grow so big? I've seen everything.

Moose, grizzly, caribou, Dall sheep...what a vacation!"

"Sheep?" asked Ashley. "When did you see sheep?"

"Yesterday, in the other plane," he answered, proudly. He'd forgotten he was the only one who had seen sheep.

Johnny nosed the floats on shore and jumped to the ground.

"We'll head west 'til we hit the shore of the second lake. I want everyone to stay close. If you get lost here, you'll probably never be found. Understood? Ashley and Matthew, keep each other in sight at all times. Jonathan, we'll do the same. If anything happens, follow the trail back to the plane and wait. You can call for help on the plane's radio."

"Where's the trail?" asked Matthew. "I don't see a trail."

"I'll show you. It was made by that moose and his friends. Where there are animals, there are trails. Once we get to the other lake, stay in the trees. Any questions?"

"They had rifles in the cave," said Ashley. She turned to Jonathan. "Are we doing the right thing?"

"Aw, Ashley," groaned Matthew. "Please don't start."

"Matthew, put a lid on it," she said, her voice firm.

Johnny Johnson noted the change in Ashley's voice. Even though he was with them, she took responsibility for her own, and Matthew's, safety. She's a born leader, he thought.

"Well?" asked Ashley.

"It's the right thing," said Jonathan. "If you're not sure, we can stay with the plane. Right, Matthew?"

"Your call, Ash," replied Matthew.

"Johnny, I'd like to go, but I'm worried," she said.

"It's your decision, Ashley," said Johnny. "No guarantees."

Ashley felt comfortable with the policeman. "Let's do it," she decided, her enthusiasm returning.

They set off through the trees. They found a trail — Johnny was right about the moose. The ground was covered with hoofprints. Johnny pointed out grizzly  tracks, but assured them the bear had passed several days ago.

Soon they came to the second lake. They could barely see the Lodge on the far side.

Matthew spotted a large bird swimming near the shore. "Ashley, look at the duck. It's huge."

"It's not a duck, Matthew, it's a loon. See its black head?"

"A loon? It looks like a big duck."

"Remember that beautiful sound we hear every night? Like a loud, echoing song of the wilderness? That's the loon. We heard it the first night at Sekulmun."

"What's it doing?" Matthew asked. The loon dove under the water and popped up a short distance away. Then it lifted its body above the water by flapping its wings faster and faster until it seemed to be standing on the surface. It was beautiful.

"I don't know why it does that," said Ashley. "I call it the loon dance."

"It's not far now," said Johnny. "Move quietly in case anyone is around."

Ashley smiled. She wondered if Johnny realized how quietly he moved through the bush. She saw Matthew copy the way Johnny walked, holding off branches with his arm rather than crashing straight through.

Johnny stopped. The others gathered round. He indicated they should be quiet.

Jonathan heard nothing. Then he began noticing sounds around them. A breeze whispered among the trees. He heard a scratching sound as a small animal scampered across a branch. Then a soft *splish* as a fish leaped for an insect that came too close.

Birds chirped as though they had been having a party all along, but no one had noticed. Amid these sounds, Jonathan noticed the stillness of four people standing together in the wilderness. Stillness is its own kind of sound, he thought. When he looked at his sister and brother, they seemed different. Then he realized they weren't different...he was just seeing them in a new way.

"There's no one around," said Johnny. "See the cabin through the trees? That's where we're going."

The abandoned trapper's cabin was run down. Bears had destroyed everything inside over the years. Mattress stuffing was scattered everywhere. Simple shelves tilted off the log walls at crazy angles. The wood stove was lying on its side.

"Nothing here," said Johnny. "Hasn't been anyone in here for a long time."

Ashley was fascinated by the crumbling sod roof. It was mossy, with wildflowers and small trees growing in it.

Johnny didn't know what to think. He was sure anyone hiding something on this side of the lake would use the cabin. He had a reputation for having a sixth sense about where people would go when running from the law in the Territory. In reality, his sixth sense came from knowing where to find old cabins like this one. He knew where to find hundreds just like it.

"Where's Matthew?" asked Ashley. *"Matthew!"*

"In here," came a muffled voice from no place at all.

Ashley hurried to where she thought the voice came from. "Matthew Adams, this is no time to be playing games. Where are you?"

Matthew climbed through the middle of a bush. "There's some kind of hole in there, and guess what?" He stood before the bush proudly.

"Matt, how do you do that?" asked Jonathan, impressed. "Did you really find something?"

Matthew merely waved them toward the bush, grinning broadly.

"I remember now," said Johnny. "The hole is a food

cache. That's where the trapper stored food. My hat's off to you, Matthew. I should have thought to look there."

They found several large wooden crates in the back of the cache. They pulled one out and pried it open.

"That's the welding equipment we saw," said Jonathan. "And those metal boxes — they were in the cavern, too."

The metal boxes were the size of a small book. Johnny slid the top from one.

"Empty," groaned Ashley. "Wouldn't you know it?"

"Let's look in another crate," urged Matthew.

The second crate held more metal boxes. These ones were welded shut. They couldn't see what was inside without cutting off the metal tops.

"Now do you believe us?" asked Matthew.

"I believed you from the start," replied Johnny. He turned the box in his hand and compared its weight to the empty one. "The welded one is heavier, so there's something inside. But what?"

"Drugs," said Ashley and Jonathan, together.

"Illegal drugs," said Matthew. "That's it...those geeks are smugglers."

"It may be drugs," said Johnny. "Everything fits a smuggling pattern. Except for one thing."

"What's the one thing?" asked Ashley.

"Why the Yukon? And why back here in the bush? There must be easier ways to smuggle drugs."

"What now?" asked Matthew. "Are you going to arrest them? Will you arrest sleazy Harry?"

"We'll go back to the detachment in Haines Junction

and have this box opened and tested. If it's an illegal substance, I'll need support to arrest these people. It's too big for one person to handle alone."

"A bust...a real drug bust!" said Matthew. "Way cool!"

They returned the crates to the cache. The hike back to the plane took no time at all. Jonathan remembered the same feeling when returning to Sekulmun Lake. The trip back from somewhere always seemed faster and easier than when he went initially. Maybe it was because being unfamiliar with a place made the first trip seem longer.

The plane was as they left it. Because the trip was a success, they were in high spirits as they fastened themselves into their seats. Johnny pushed the plane away from shore and leaped aboard.

"Everyone strapped in?" he asked.

"Roger," announced Matthew.

The engine rattled to life and the nose prop whirled. Johnny guided the plane onto the lake and circled for takeoff. At the precise moment the floats lifted from the water, an explosion rocked the rear of the plane. Behind her Ashley saw daylight — the tail of the plane had disappeared!

The aircraft lurched to the left and its wing tip knifed the water. The Cessna flipped on its back as easily as a maple leaf in a brisk wind. Their seatbelts held them in as gravity and the plane's motion tried to throw them into the lake.

The mayhem lasted only a heartbeat...then ceased. They were now upside down in a sinking airplane. Johnny knew they wouldn't stay afloat for long. His seatbelt held him upside down, blood trickling across his forehead.

He had to get the kids out. Grabbing the bottom of his seat, he pulled himself up and unfastened his seatbelt. He tried not to move too much...shifting his weight might cause the plane to go under.

"I'm OK," said Jonathan, his frightened voice barely a whisper. "Ashley's not moving. I have to get out...you have to help me, Johnny. Ashley isn't moving!"

Johnny unhooked Jonathan's seatbelt and lowered him to the ceiling. They released Ashley and Matthew. Ashley opened her eyes...she was only dazed. The plane was filling with water and the tail was sinking.

"I'm going to open the door and we're going to get out *right now,*" said Johnny. He forced the door open with brute strength and put Matthew on the wing. Taking Ashley in his arms, he jumped into the icy water. Jonathan followed.

Matthew saw they had drifted close to shore. He yelled to the others and pointed in the direction they should go. He knew they could only swim for a few minutes before the cold water drained their energy. He dove into the lake. When his head popped above the surface, his arms were already moving.

"Follow me!" he yelled.

They heard him and swam for their lives.

11

FAST FREDDY

Once safely on shore, they assessed their injuries. In addition to the cut on his forehead, Johnny had a broken arm and sore ribs. Ashley made it to shore on her own, but she still felt groggy. Johnny thought she might have a slight concussion. Jonathan and Matthew escaped without injury.

They lit a small fire in a clearing away from the shore. Once they recovered from the shock, the effects of their time in the water took hold. They began to shake uncontrollably. The warmth of the fire became the most important thing in the world.

"Ashley," said Johnny, "sit down here while you're drying out. You took a nasty bump on your head. We'll stay here for a while." Ashley looked better, but Johnny didn't want to take chances.

"What happened?" asked Matthew.

"I don't know," replied Johnny. "I've never seen anything like it." With Jonathan's help he worked at putting a splint on his arm.

"It was a bomb," said Ashley. She wasn't suggesting it was a bomb — she was saying it *was* a bomb.

"I think so, too," said Matthew. "It didn't sound like it was part of the plane. It was a separate thing. Is there part of the plane that could blow up like that, Jonathan?"

"Not in the back end. Fire, maybe, but not an explosion. Did you have anything stored in the rear, Johnny? Flares, maybe?"

"Nothing that could do that." Until now he didn't realize Jonathan knew about airplanes. "Do you fly, Jonathan?"

"Yes."

"He's an airplane freak," said Ashley. "Anything you want to know about airplanes, just ask Jonathan."

"It must have been a bomb," said Matthew, ignoring the others. "They must have put it in the plane when we went to the other lake."

"And exploded it with a timing device," said Ashley.

"It probably wasn't a timing device," said Matthew. "They didn't know when we'd be back."

"Remote control," said Jonathan. "All they had to do was wait until they saw us take off — then push the button. But they pushed it a bit too early."

"These people are sick," said Ashley. "They must be doing something really serious if they'd try to kill us."

"I should have been more careful," said Johnny. "The

84

last thing I should have done was endanger your lives."

"Dad says if you're not willing to take some risks, life probably isn't worth living," said Matthew.

Johnny laughed. Hearing such words from a young boy made their truth stand out.

"That's true, but as a police officer, I have a special responsibility to show good judgment. I shouldn't put you at risk."

"Not according to Dad," replied Jonathan. "We're the ones who decided to come. Dad says if people are afraid to take risks they become slaves to doing nothing."

"I'm glad you brought us," said Ashley. "At least you gave us the option."

"What are we going to do, Johnny?" asked Matthew. "We're stuck here with no food and no way out."

"Yeah," said Jonathan, "and we lost the evidence from the cache. Now they'll move the stuff and we won't be able to prove anything."

"Don't worry about that," said Johnny, patting his vest pocket. "I still have the box. Those people are going to jail. Count on it."

"But how do we get out?" asked Ashley.

"We'll walk," announced Johnny. "We're going to walk right on down to Fast Freddy's place for hot dogs, hamburgers and fries."

"Fast Freddy's?" asked Matthew. "You mean Fast Freddy the gold miner?"

Johnny gave Matthew a questioning look. "Yes, Matthew, the one and only. How did you know?" He was surprised and impressed.

"In the plane to Silver City Marty talked about Fast Freddy and his wife being sick and his boy helping him at the mine."

Johnny explained there was a horse trail that hadn't been used for many years leading from Gladstone Lakes right to Fast Freddy's placer claim. They could borrow a truck from Freddy and drive to Haines Junction for help.

"What's a placer claim?" asked Ashley.

"Placer mining is surface mining," explained Johnny. "They don't dig tunnels into the ground like in underground mining. They load surface material on a conveyor belt and sift the gold out. That's what Fast Freddy does."

"Why is he called Fast Freddy?" asked Matthew.

"You'll see," said Johnny, smiling broadly.

HOT DOGS, HAMBURGERS AND FRIES

The hike to Fast Freddy's was difficult. They found the horse trail, but it was overgrown with bushes and often blocked by large fallen trees. After hours of hard walking, the land flattened out and they found themselves walking across low hills with few trees.

"We should be about five miles from Fast Freddy's," said Johnny, pausing for a break. "After that, it's a couple of hours to the highway and less than an hour to the Junction. We have plenty of daylight left."

The hills had a gold-colored sheen in the afternoon sun. Jonathan and Ashley gazed across miles of wilderness.

Snow-covered mountain peaks provided a backdrop no matter which way they looked.

"It's like being on the roof of the world," said Ashley.

"Can you imagine how many centuries have passed with everything staying pretty much as we see it right now?" said Jonathan. "It's so calm and beautiful and so danger-ous at the same time. I'm glad Dad brought us up North. It's a special place." He threw his arm around Ashley's shoulder and followed Johnny toward Fast Freddy's claim.

They heard the sound of a motor before they saw anything.

"That's Freddy running his Bobcat," said Johnny.

"His what?" asked Matthew.

"A small front-end loader he uses to load dirt onto the conveyor belt. Like a small tractor."

They soon came upon the machine chugging slowly along the gravel beside a creek. At the controls sat a small man who didn't seem surprised to see them. He shut the motor off.

"Afternoon, Fred," said Johnny. "Looks like you're working hard."

"Always workin' hard, Johnny," the old man replied. "Good day for it, too." He looked at the children. "Who ya got here? How ya doin' kids? Who do they belong to, Johnny?"

"Visitors from California. Meet Ashley, Jonathan, and Matthew Adams from Palm Springs."

"Palm Springs? Lord Almighty. I been there...desert, eh? Went to Arizona one winter, too. Real hot. You're a long way from home, by golly."

The old man spoke so slowly they weren't sure if he was finished. He continued: "Let me get off this thing and we'll go over to the trailer for coffee." Climbing slowly from his seat, he stepped to the ground, using a cane for support. "You kids go ahead. The trailer's open and my boy Walter's there. Tell him we'll be along in a few minutes."

It became clear why they called him Fast Freddy. He moved like a glacier — slower than slow. Every step was in slow motion.

Walter welcomed them. He seemed happy to have company. He moved almost as slowly as his father.

"Saw you coming...come in and have some pie."

"Are you really going to be seventy-two?" asked Matthew, claiming a spot at the table.

"Matthew," Ashley blurted, "when are you going to learn?"

"That's OK, young lady," said Walter, smiling. "You're right, sonny, I'm seventy-two next week. My father's older than that, though. What kind of pie would you like? We have apple, apple and apple. Homemade from Angela's Donut Shop. Fresh last week."

"Outstanding!" said Matthew. "Apple sounds perfect."

Walter told them how the gold mining process worked. He even showed them a nugget found a few days earlier. It was as big as Matthew's fist and looked like a nugget people find in their dreams.

They told him about their adventures and about the

explosion in the plane.

"You don't say!" Walter exclaimed. "That's the best tale I ever heard. Better than when the park warden was caught poachin' a moose a few years back."

Fast Freddy and Johnny finally appeared. Freddy was happy to lend them his four wheel drive truck for the drive to Haines Junction.

"We should go right away," said Johnny. "It's getting late." He pointed to his broken arm. "Can either of you drive a truck?"

Ashley and Jonathan nodded. "We can drive," said Jonathan.

"Why don't you give it a try until we get to the highway? You drive, Jonathan. Ashley has a nasty bump on her head. I'll be all right with one arm once we're on the highway. It takes two hands to drive on the mining road."

Jonathan was thrilled. He was surprised at being treated with such respect. Most adults didn't think teenagers could do anything properly. All it takes is a little respect, he thought.

They thanked Fast Freddy and Walter for their help and started down the muddy track only a miner would call a road.

"Hey," said Matthew, remembering something. "I didn't

find out why you said we'd have hot dogs, hamburgers and fries at Fast Freddy's."

Johnny laughed. "It's a local joke." He pointed to a large tree just ahead. "That tree is where Fast Freddy's claim starts. When we get there, look at the sign nailed on the other side."

At the tree Jonathan stopped the truck.

WELCOME TO FAST FREDDY'S!
HOT DOGS, HAMBURGERS AND FRIES!
SOFT ICE CREAM!
ALL MAJOR CREDIT CARDS ACCEPTED!

Everyone had a good laugh. The sign conveyed the friendliness they had found in the trailer. Ashley was beginning to think Yukon people were as special as the North itself.

12

THE COMMANDING OFFICER

I n the Haines Junction R.C.M.P. detachment the next morning, Johnny Johnson related events of the previous day to his commanding officer. The metal box was cut open. It contained two pounds of high grade heroin. The atmosphere was electric. Word of the plane's explosion had spread from officer to officer and excitement was building.

The man in charge listened to their story. The heroin, wrapped in a plastic bag, lay on his desk.

"You children have shown initiative and independence," he said. "On behalf of the Force I'd like to thank you for bringing this operation to our attention."

Ashley and Jonathan could see he wasn't happy they were involved. His voice was tight and his face tense as he thanked them.

"We called Sacramento. Your father will be gone for at least two more days. We let him know where you are." He turned to Johnny.

"We have enough evidence to raid the Lodge, but we have to look at the bigger picture. We still don't know how they get the heroin to the Lodge or even into the country. We don't know what they do with it once they get it. We need to know more so we can nail the kingpins."

"True," agreed Johnny. "On the other hand, they tried to kill us yesterday by sabotaging the plane. They know we're on to them, so they won't hang around."

"Don't worry, they aren't going anywhere. We have people watching every move they make. Everyone leaving the Yukon is having their identification checked. Keep in mind they may think you didn't make it yesterday. They may think they're safe."

"If that's true," said Johnny, "we may still be able to discover how they operate."

"Of course, Johnny, *you* won't be on the case for a while," said his boss. "If they find out you're alive, they'll stop everything for sure. You'll stay at the motel until things settle down. We'll bring meals and anything you need. Same thing for the children."

Ashley was shocked. "What? You're putting us in a motel? You're incarcerating *us*?"

"Afraid so, Miss Adams. They may try to harm you and your brothers. This is a dangerous situation. I'm sorry."

Ashley knew it was true. Still, she thought he should ask if they would mind staying in a motel.

"Sir," said Jonathan, quietly, "we appreciate the danger and your desire to keep us safe. On the other hand, if you think we should spend the rest of our vacation cooped up in a motel room, couldn't you ask if we agree?"

Ashley, Matthew and Jonathan glared at the commanding officer. Johnny Johnson covered a grin with his hand. The boss grew red with anger.

"You damn kids have caused enough trouble. What kind of father leaves his children alone in the wilderness, anyway? I don't want you running around my jurisdiction getting hurt. Constable Johnson, get these kids over to the motel and keep them there until I order their release. On second thought, I'll get someone else to take them over." He was getting uptight. He turned to Jonathan.

"I'll station an officer at your door. I don't want any screw-ups. Kids your age should show obedience and respect."

Jonathan and Ashley were getting steamed. "Obedience is for sheep and respect is something you earn," shot back Jonathan. "You don't get respect just because you wear a uniform."

The color in the man's face grew a deeper red. He hit the intercom button and had his secretary hustle them from his office. He was being judged by a couple of kids, and he was angry.

The motel room was better than expected. It had a television and refrigerator. Matthew thought the TV was great because it was hooked to a satellite dish and received more than a hundred stations.

Their watchdog, as Ashley called him, brought them a lunch of hamburgers and fries. When Ashley asked if they were from Fast Freddy's Diner, he looked at her blankly. The rest of the day he sat in his patrol car drumming his fingers on the steering wheel in time with music only he could hear.

Ashley and Jonathan weren't enjoying this part of their vacation. When it started raining late in the afternoon, they felt trapped and miserable. Evening brought darker skies and pelting rain. A summer storm had moved into Haines Junction.

"Matthew, how can you sit there watching baseball?" asked Ashley. "Why don't you give it a rest?"

Matthew had heard this complaint many times before. "And do what?"

"Anything but watch baseball."

"Such as? Lighten up, Ash. It's the Angels and Yankees." The Angels were his favorite team because he had watched them in spring training in Palm Springs when he was younger.

"What's the score?" asked Jonathan.

"Not sure," replied Matthew, absently.

"You *never* know the score," sighed Ashley. "Where do you go when you watch TV, Matthew? What kind of cyberspace are you in?"

Matthew let his mind unfuzz. "Why don't we just take off? I'll bet we could get out easily. Sgt. Preston outside our door is no obstacle."

"I agree," said Jonathan. "He sits out there and we sit

in here. It's mega-stupid."

"What would we do?" asked Ashley. "We can't walk back to Sekulmun Lake and we have no transportation."

"We could borrow a car," suggested Matthew.

"Oh, right, Matthew," shot back Ashley. "I'm sure. Too cool. Why don't we hijack a motorhome? At least we'd be comfortable for the ten minutes we were free. Then we could wait for Dad in a real jail."

"Chill, Ash," said Matthew. "What's your idea?"

"Man," sighed Jonathan, "maybe I shouldn't have said what I did to that bozo in the office. Maybe he'd have been more reasonable if I'd..."

Ashley interrupted. "No way, Jonathan. The guy's a Neanderthal. He wasn't going to change his mind. He's the kind who has to be right. Changing his mind would mean he was weak. What you said was true." She smiled at some inner joke. "Man, did you diss him good. He was *so* ticked!"

"Yeah, Jonathan," said Matthew, "you sure yanked his chain. I could imagine Dad clapping when you dissed him. It's weird...he's the first Yukon person we've met who's a total jerk. He didn't even want to admit we helped find the heroin. Maybe he doesn't like kids...or Americans."

"Listen," said Ashley. "I hear something." It was a soft thumping sound.

"In the bathroom," said Matthew. "There's someone at the window."

They raced to the bathroom. The window was made of frosted glass, so they couldn't see who, or what, was outside.

"Open the window," said a muffled voice.

Matthew climbed on the toilet seat and tried to release the latch. Ashley grabbed his arm, stopping him.

"Who's there?" she asked.

"It's me...Johnny Johnson. Open the window."

Matthew succeeded in turning the latch and pulled the window open.

With some difficulty, a soaking wet Johnny Johnson climbed into their bathroom. "Hi, team. I thought you'd never hear me."

"What's happening?" asked Matthew, happy to see their friend. "What are you doing here?"

"Sit down and I'll explain," said Johnny. "Are you ready to do more investigating?"

"*Are* we?" asked Jonathan. "Anything beats sitting in here."

"What about your boss?" asked Ashley. She was as happy as the others to see Johnny, but she felt they shouldn't rush into anything without thinking.

"I'm really sorry about what happened today," began Johnny. "You kids deserve more respect than that. Let me try to explain." Johnny fixed a cup of coffee.

"Our commanding officer was posted up here only a few months ago. He's from Ottawa...from Headquarters. He has no experience doing real police work, but he has degrees in criminology and sociology. He doesn't know what it's like to arrest drunk drivers or pull injured people from car wrecks." Johnny paused, choosing his words carefully.

"He's full of theories about how to run the detachment, but he has a lot to learn about the North. Of course, *he* doesn't think he has anything to learn. He's about to cost us nabbing these crooks...he just doesn't appreciate how the Yukon is different from other places. It's not easy to stop people from leaving here. The Territory's too big and there are too many ways to get out. But he doesn't get it."

"You'll lose your job," said Ashley. "If you do anything, he'll fire you."

"Maybe," said Johnny. "But if he fires me, he'll have to fire everyone. We're all working together."

"Like a mutiny?" asked Ashley. "What do we do now?"

"Grab your stuff and I'll tell you on the way."

"What about Sgt. Preston?" asked Jonathan.

"He'll report you missing tomorrow. By then it won't matter. Let's go."

Johnny helped them through the window and led them to a truck parked nearby. The truck was packed with camping gear and was pulling a trailer loaded with two all-terrain vehicles. The presence of the ATV's hinted they were in for some real back country adventure.

SUMMER SNOW

Once on the highway Johnny explained they were returning to Gladstone Lakes the same way they had come out a day earlier — except this time they would drive the ATV's. He wanted to personally keep an eye on Harry, Leo and Gurder.

"We can't stop them from leaving if they really want to go. The Yukon has more than 180,000 square miles. It's not a place where you casually keep an eye on people. You have to watch them real close. That's reality. But the boss doesn't get it."

"Maybe he doesn't respect your ideas because you're Indian," said Matthew. "Like he dissed us because we're kids."

Johnny was surprised by Matthew's insight. "What does *dissed* mean?"

"Disrespected," answered Ashley. "Like Matthew is disrespecting people lately with his attitude. Matthew, you have to be more subtle. Some things you just shouldn't say."

"What's wrong with what I said?" asked Matthew. "What does subtle mean?"

"It's OK, Ashley," said Johnny. "He's only being honest. We could do with more of it these days. It's a lost virtue."

"That's what Dad says," said Matthew. "Dad says the very same thing, Ashley. How am I supposed to learn things if I'm not allowed to talk about them?"

They drove through the pelting rain. Soon they pulled off the highway and started down a rough road. A sign said SILVER CITY.

"Is Silver City a real city?" asked Jonathan.

"Not anymore," replied Johnny. "Back around 1903, when Dawson Charlie found gold in Silver Creek, there was a roadhouse here, an old-time motel. A fair-sized settlement grew, but it's only a ghost town now."

Before reaching Silver City they turned onto the old mining road. Driving out the previous night had been slow, but now they moved even more slowly because they were pulling the trailer. The heavy rain made the road slippery and the creeks they crossed were rising fast. Ashley could see Johnny's concern as he drove along narrow, dangerous ridges.

"We might have trouble getting up to Fast Freddy's. Hope you don't mind a little work. We'll have to winch through some bad spots. I'm not much good with this cast on my arm."

"We'll get through," said Matthew. "We have to...the Mounties always get their man, right?"

"Or their woman," added Ashley. Everyone laughed.

They were climbing steadily into the mountains when the rain stopped. Johnny didn't get a chance to turn the windshield wipers off, however. In place of rain, the wipers began sweeping away large white snowflakes. Johnny cursed their bad luck. He stopped the truck to check the road. Everyone jumped out.

"*Snow!*" screamed Ashley. "Real live snow. It's the middle of summer and it's snowing everywhere!"

"Awesome," said Jonathan. "Outstanding. Can you believe this? It's a snowstorm!"

Matthew said nothing. He was enchanted. He spread his arms to the sky as though trying to touch every snowflake before it hit the ground. He turned in circles, gazing into the millions of fluffy crystals hurtling at him from above.

Johnny wasn't enthusiastic. "Yes, it's snow, all right. I'm afraid the spirits aren't on our side tonight. We may not reach Fast Freddy's if this keeps up."

"Oh, Johnny, the spirits are *definitely* on our side tonight," said Ashley. "This is so beautiful...so romantic! I wish Dad could see it." She looked totally alive.

"In the truck, team," said Johnny. "If we don't keep moving we may be stuck here all night. C'mon, Matthew. You'll see plenty of snow in the next little while."

At several points Ashley and Jonathan had to get out and guide Johnny along cliffs because he couldn't see the road. They were nervous just standing on the road, let alone driving on it. The only reassuring thing was Johnny's calm approach to everything. If they had to be here, he was the man to be with.

They finally made it to Fast Freddy's camp. The famous welcome sign was covered by wind-blown snow. Pulling up to the trailer, Johnny knew something was wrong. Freddy's truck, which had been returned that day, was nowhere in sight. A different truck, with a cabover camper, sat in its place. There was no sign of life.

"Stay here and keep your heads down. Something's wrong. I'm going to check the trailer."

Johnny drew his revolver and moved toward the dark trailer. Snow still fell. Everything was too quiet.

Johnny stopped and listened. All he heard was the wind.

13

FAST FREDDY'S II

J ohnny circled the trailer. He opened the door a crack and listened. His senses tingled. He knew there was someone inside, but he heard nothing.

"Anyone there? Freddy? Walter? It's me, Johnny Johnson."

Grunts came from the trailer. Johnny's flashlight illuminated several bound and gagged figures. He yelled for the others to join him as he untied the captives.

"What happened?"

"Visitors," answered Walter. "Your friends from the Lodge. Harry and his goons busted in and tied us up. Thought we were dead ducks, but they didn't hurt us." Walter rubbed his arms to get the blood circulating. "You all right, Pa?"

"I'm good, son," replied the old man. "A hell of a lot

better than them terrorists are gonna be when I catch 'em."

"Stuck guns in our faces, just like in the movies," said Walter. "They have a surprise comin' when we get in their faces — and it won't be with guns, either."

"Calm down," said Johnny. "Tell me what happened."

"We were havin' coffee with these folks when they barged in and took over," said Freddy. "Johnny, this is Mark, his wife Linda, and Bob. They stopped by to visit. Anyway, they poked around outside and then stole our pickup and Bob's ATV's. Took off into the bush. That's it."

Walter turned his attention to the children. "Hello, again."

"Hi, Walter," said Matthew.

"Did they steal your big nugget?" asked Ashley.

"Hell, no!" replied Walter. "We hide our gold pretty good. They weren't lookin' to steal gold, though. They were just tryin' to get away."

"You keep flashin' that nugget around, we're gonna have more unwelcome visitors," said Freddy.

"How long ago were they here?" asked Johnny.

"A few hours," said Freddy. "You didn't see our truck when you drove in, did you?"

"No. I suppose they're headed for Skagway or Haines. Maybe up to Anchorage. I sure wish I'd come out here earlier."

"If they were going to Skagway, Haines or Anchorage, why would they take ATV's?" asked Matthew. "It doesn't make sense. There are highways to those places."

102

"Smart boy," said Fast Freddy. "You're right. It's too much trouble haulin' those things out for no good reason."

Ashley was puzzled. Why would they take the all-terrain vehicles? For insurance in case the truck got stuck? The truck had a winch, so that wasn't the reason. Why *did* they take them? A light suddenly came on in her mind.

"I know their plan. They aren't going anywhere. At least, not far. They're going to hide in the Yukon until things cool off. Then they can leave without a hassle."

"You may be right, Ashley," said Johnny. "Harry and Gurder don't know the area, but Leo does. He knows every trapping cabin and ghost town in the Territory."

"Coulda' hid the truck and took off on the ATV's," suggested Freddy.

"Could have rolled the truck into a gully or a lake," said Walter.

"Where would they go?" Ashley asked.

"Plenty of places," said Freddy. "Plenty of places."

Johnny's face lit up. "Kloo Lake! That's where Leo would take them. To the old settlement at Kloo Lake."

"Johnny," said Walter, "the trail to Kloo Lake is impossible to drive at this time of year, even on ATV's. Too much swamp...too soft."

"That's what Leo is counting on us to think," replied Johnny. "It's been cold the past few nights so the ground's harder. It would be real work, but they could get in. Once there, they could wait until we stopped looking. It's a good idea."

"Let's go after them!" said Matthew.

"It's late," said Johnny. "In the morning we can work out a plan. There's a lot to consider. How would you like some more company for the night, Fred? Walter?"

GHOST TOWN

In the morning they walked along the mining road to where the old trail to Kloo Lake began. Snow remained, but bright sun promised a return to summer temperatures by afternoon.

There was no sign of the truck. Matthew found broken branches near the road — probably broken by the ATV's. A more intensive search soon uncovered the pickup. It had been driven through a gap in the trees and pushed into a deep gully.

"We have them now," concluded Matthew.

"Not yet," said Johnny. "There's still work to do."

"What are you going to do?" asked Matthew. "Can we help?"

"Since you kids started this investigation, you should have a chance to help finish it," said Johnny.

"They have guns," said Ashley. "It might be dangerous."

"Not if we're careful," replied Johnny. "And if you do what I tell you. It's your choice. Bob, Mark and Linda have to go back to town."

"What about getting the kingpins?" asked Jonathan.

"Too late. They've already abandoned the operation. If we can catch these guys, they'll tell us how they move the heroin in and out of the Yukon. Freddy and Walter have a few ideas that might help."

"You better get a move-on while the ground's cold, else you won't get in," said Walter.

Ashley and Jonathan decided to go with Johnny.

The four-wheeled ATV's Johnny had brought were easy to drive. Their way was easier than expected because  Harry and his friends had already removed the bigger trees lying across the trail. They made slow but steady progress. Stopping for a break, Johnny pointed to where they were going.

"An hour from here. We won't drive right in because they'd hear the machines. There are a dozen good cabins they could use, but I think I can guess which one they're in. We'll sneak up on them by going through the cemetery. They won't expect it."

"Cemetery?" asked Ashley, her face showing disapproval.

"Cemetery," repeated Johnny. "An old Indian cemetery where many of my ancestors are buried."

"Do we have to go through a cemetery, Johnny?" persisted Ashley.

"Yes," he said. "You'll see why when we get there."

Once close to the abandoned settlement they began walking. Jonathan and Ashley carried shotguns. They had been trained to use firearms and had participated in shooting competitions. Tracking down drug smugglers, however, wasn't what their father had in mind when he enrolled them in classes.

They moved quickly through the trees. Matthew stayed close to Johnny, aware this was serious business. They soon stood at the edge of a large clearing. Dilapidated log buildings were everywhere. Some were large, some small; all were in the final stages of ruin. Beyond them was Kloo Lake. Johnny scanned the area with his binoculars. He saw wisps of smoke rising from one of the cabins.

"Just as I thought," he whispered. "They're in the big cabin on the far right. We'll circle through the trees. Remember, they'll still be nervous, so they may be watching."

They circled the clearing, staying well back among the trees. Johnny led them to a point at the edge of the clearing behind the cabin. One of the men, who had stepped outside, could be heard talking.

"If you don't like it here, Harry, you can get lost. If you don't quit complaining, I'm going to throw you in the lake so you'll really have something to complain about."

"That's Leo," whispered Matthew.

"It's Leo, all right," confirmed Johnny. "Now we know where two of them are, but where's Gurder?"

Ashley tapped Johnny on the shoulder.

"What's that?" she asked, pointing to dozens of minia-ture houses lying between them and the cabin. They looked like small playhouses and were complete in every detail. Since they were only three feet tall, Ashley knew they weren't playhouses. Besides, there were too many.

"That's the cemetery," said Johnny. "Those are *spirit houses.* They're for each person's spirit. Their spirit lives in the house after death."

"They're so elaborate," said Jonathan.

"Wow," said Matthew.

"Do you mean someone is buried under each of those little houses?" asked Ashley. "It's so weird."

"Not really," said Johnny. "Our people believe a person's spirit never dies so it always needs a place to live. We provide the spirit a place to live."

"Cool," said Matthew. "When I die, I'd like one of those for my spirit."

"Creepy," said Ashley. "Johnny, I'm not walking through there. I mean, it's a cemetery. I'm not walking through it."

"That's OK. You stay here. I'll sneak up behind the cabin and look through the window. If they're all there and I think we can surprise them, I'll wave for Jonathan and Matthew to join me. Ashley, load your shotgun in case there's trouble. Stay out of sight."

Johnny worked his way to the cabin by moving from one spirit house to the next. When he was close enough, he heard the three men arguing.

"Sit down, Gurder," yelled Harry. "If I want you to make his face into pizza, I'll tell you. Right now I want to know how we're going to stay here without losing our minds. Damn it! We should've flown out after we blew up that plane."

"Easy to say now," said Leo. "Don't forget you thought

we were in the clear when we blasted the plane. You only decided to leave after our cop snitch warned us we were being watched. Face reality, Harry. If you don't do this right, you won't get to retire on the Riviera. You'll be vacationing in the penitentiary."

Harry lost all pretense of being a gentleman. Without his fancy Lodge, his sleazy nature showed through.

"You think you're so damn smart, Leo," he shouted. "The longer we hide out here, the harder it's going to be to get out."

Johnny knew this was a perfect time to catch them off guard. The three men weren't even carrying guns. He waved for Jonathan and Matthew. The arguing in the cabin continued.

"I'll go around to the front door with Jonathan," Johnny whispered. "Matthew, you stay here. Jonathan, when I go through the door, you stay back, just outside the door. Is your gun loaded?"

Jonathan nodded.

Johnny and Jonathan circled the cabin in a crouched position. Without hesitating, Johnny burst through the door, pistol drawn.

"*R.C.M.P.!* Put your hands in the air! Hands in the air and up against the wall! *Move!*"

There was instant confusion. Harry and Leo froze, but Gurder lunged for a pistol on the table. Without hesitating, Johnny fired a shot over the big German's head. Gurder froze.

"That's a warning. Next one who moves gets shot."

Johnny's voice was calm and steady. They knew he wasn't bluffing.

"Jonathan, get in here. Point your shotgun at the big guy. Forget the others. If he moves, shoot."

Johnny collected the assortment of rifles and pistols the men had with them.

"Matthew, come in here," he ordered. Matthew appeared in the doorway. "Take these weapons one at a time and throw them in the lake. Be careful, they're loaded."

Matthew did as instructed. He was amazed how the friendly Johnny Johnson transformed into a tough, efficient cop in front of his eyes. Matthew was almost afraid of him.

"Hey!" yelled Gurder, staring at Jonathan. "The kid's shakin'...he's gonna shoot me by accident."

"You OK, Jonathan?" asked Johnny.

"I think so," he replied.

"Good. Relax your muscles. Don't worry about shaking. If he moves, pull the trigger. He's a killer."

The big man knew when to quit. He had a better chance of getting let off by a judge than he had of getting away from Johnny Johnson.

Johnny herded the captives to the ATV's they had stolen from Bob. Gurder and Leo were told to drive slowly to where Johnny had left his own ATV's. Harry was ordered to walk. When they reached their machines, Ashley was waiting.

"Ashley," said Johnny, "these men are desperate criminals. They'll be looking to escape on the way to Fast Freddy's. I want you to show them you can use your shotgun."

"Really?" asked Ashley.

"Really," confirmed Johnny.

"OK. Matthew, get a can of soda from my pack and give it to the big guy."

Matthew got the soda and casually tossed it to Gurder.

"Throw it in the air," instructed Ashley.

Gurder hurled the can high in the air. Johnny and Jonathan kept their eyes on the prisoners as the can spun above the trees.

A shot rang out. *Blam!*

"You hit it!" yelled Matthew.

Blam!

"Hit it *again!*" squealed Matthew.

Ashley lowered the gun and reloaded. She looked at Gurder. The fight left his eyes.

"Time to visit Freddy and Walter," said Johnny, a big smile creasing his face. "They want to talk to you fellows."

14

THE CONFESSION

The trip to Fast Freddy's proceeded without incident. Ashley's sharpshooting convinced Gurder and the others to behave.

Johnny admired the youngsters. They were confident, but not overconfident. They knew their capabilities and their limitations. He looked forward to meeting their father. Before reaching the trail's turnoff, Johnny called them to a halt.

"Ashley, go on ahead to the mining road. When we come to it, I want everyone to turn right, toward Freddy's trailer. Make sure they turn that way."

When they came to the road, they were met by Fast Freddy and Walter.

"Never saw such a thing, Johnny," said Walter. "You and these kids make a good team."

"Thanks, Walter. They held up their end, that's a fact." He watched Fast Freddy lead the caravan along the road. "Walter, look at your father...he's walking as fast as everyone else."

Walter chuckled. "Sure he is. He moves slow because he wants to move slow. There's nothing wrong with him... never has been. He just likes to go at his own pace. Says people are in too much of a hurry to get nowhere. He's movin' faster now 'cause he's excited."

At the trailer Johnny handcuffed the prisoners.

"What now?" asked Ashley.

"These men are going to tell us how their smuggling ring works," replied Johnny.

"In your face," sneered Gurder.

"You mean in Bonanza's face, don't you?" asked Johnny. Gurder did not reply. "Is old Bonanza still around these parts, Fred?"

"Yep, that ole' grizzly still comes by, waitin' for us to drop our guard. She's dangerous, but she still tells us where the gold is."

"A grizzly bear tells you where to find gold?" asked Ashley.

"Wherever that bear sits, that's where we find gold. Ain't that just somethin'?"

"What do you think would happen if we tied Harry to your Bobcat and put a big juicy moose steak at his feet?" asked Johnny. "Think Bonanza might pay us a visit?"

"Sure she would," said Freddy. "Got caribou steaks if you want."

Freddy may have been over ninety, but you couldn't tell from looking at his eyes. They twinkled like stars in the Northern sky.

"Let's do it," said Johnny. "Come on, Harry, you're going outside. I hope you like bears."

"You won't do it," sneered Harry. "Mounties don't pull stunts. If you did, you'd lose your job. So quit bluffing. Just take us to jail and give us a decent meal." He wasn't worried.

Johnny led Harry to the Bobcat.

"Harry, you're going to tell me all about your drug smuggling ring. After you give me the information, I'm taking you to jail. I'll take you to jail even though you blew up my plane and almost killed three kids. If you don't tell me what I want to know, you're going to jail in pieces. It's up to you."

"I have rights!" said Harry.

"Correction, Harry. You *had* rights. You gave up your rights when you blew up my plane."

"Gurder blew up the plane!" blurted the little man.

"Don't worry, Harry. Gurder gets to play with Bonanza after she finishes with you."

Johnny handcuffed Harry to the front-end loader. His hands were tied behind him but his feet were left free.

"I know it'll be hard not to kick old Bonanza when she's sniffing your feet, Harry, but try not to. It'll only make her mad." He put the steak at Harry's feet.

They watched from the trailer, waiting to see if the grizzly would be attracted by the meat. For half an hour they waited and Bonanza didn't show. This didn't seem to bother Johnny. Finally, Fast Freddy sniffed the air excitedly.

"She's here," he announced. "Walter, can you see her?"

"She's here, all right," confirmed Walter. "She smells the meat. We're gonna have a hell of a time keepin' her away after she gets a few bites of Harry and Gurder."

They watched a huge blonde-colored grizzly bear amble slowly toward the meat — and Harry.

"Scram!" yelled Harry.

The bear paused, as though considering the threat.

"Get out of here you stinking beast!" screamed Harry.

The bear moved forward.

"Johnny Johnson! You'd better stop this damn bear!" Harry was worried. Had he misjudged the kind of man Johnny really was?

The bear sniffed the meat. With a huge paw she slapped the steak right into Harry's legs. With her other paw she retrieved it, tearing a long claw through his pant leg.

Harry was screaming wildly. When the claw cut into his leg, his foot kicked out reflexively and struck the bear's snout. Harry was ready to talk.

Harry's eyes were filled with terror as Johnny led him back to the trailer. He didn't even hear the shots Johnny fired to scare the bear away. Freddy offered coffee, but Harry's hands shook so much he couldn't hold the cup.

"You made a good decision, Harry," said Johnny. "I appreciate your willingness to help. Tell me about your operation. After you tell me everything, I'll deliver you to Haines Junction. Bonanza never goes into the Junction."

Harry knew he was signing his own death warrant if he spoke. However, he could still smell the bear. He was trapped.

"Where does the heroin come from?" asked Johnny.

"Europe...it comes from Germany."

"Germany?" It was not what Johnny Johnson expected.

"Yes, Germany. From a mountain-climbing club. We only handle things on this end."

"Keep talking."

"As you know," began Harry, "hundreds of climbers from all over the world come here to climb Mount Logan, Mount Kennedy and the other peaks in the Wrangell-St. Elias Range. Many come from Europe. This big club in Germany sends large groups. The heroin comes into Canada with the climbers' equipment."

"The climbers bring it in?" asked Johnny.

"No. The climbers don't know about it. It's hidden in their sleeping bags, their crampons, ascenders, axes, sleds, backpack frames — everything's been modified to conceal heroin. It's not in every piece, but it's always in some. We have codes to tell us where to look." Harry paused, afraid to go on, but afraid to stop.

"When a climb is planned, the equipment is shipped to Toronto. It's then shipped to Whitehorse where we pick it up and take it to Silver City. Before the climbers arrive, we take it to the Lodge at Gladstone, remove the heroin and repair the equipment. It's back at Silver City when the climbers arrive. They never know it happened."

Johnny couldn't believe it. "How does the equipment clear Canadian customs? They have dogs to sniff out drugs in Toronto."

"Government greed," replied Harry. "When they started charging climbers big money for expeditions, the fees became an important source of revenue. As long as the climbers kept coming, the government kept increasing fees. It's very profitable." Harry fidgeted nervously. It was clear he didn't want to blow the scheme wide open. But he had no choice.

"A few years ago customs agents in Toronto delayed a team's equipment because they thought some foil-wrapped dehydrated food looked suspicious. Because of the delay, the team couldn't make their climb. The group included a European prince and his influential friends. They were mad as hell and complained to the Canadian government. They said if you're going to charge big fees, don't mess around with our equipment. Because of the stink, customs agents were seriously hassled. Since then you can put anything in climbers' equipment and the agents won't even look at it."

"So that's when the smuggling started?"

"That's when it started. The smugglers put up the money to build the Lodge. It was designed as a front for the heroin connection."

"What do you do with the heroin after you seal it in the metal containers?"

"Listen," said Harry, regaining his composure. "If I tell

116

you everything, I won't have anything left to bargain with. I can use this information to bargain my way out of a long prison sentence. Don't forget, I'm not the boss of this operation."

"True," agreed Johnny. "Your only problem is Bonanza. She isn't much of a bargainer. If you want to try, I'll get another steak."

"Ha, ha. Very funny," said Harry, sarcastically. "You're crazy, you know, Johnny. You're loco."

"What do you do with the heroin?" repeated Johnny.

"Hide it in motorhomes. People coming to the Lodge park their motorhomes at Silver City. We usually take off the gas tank, cut a hole in it and hide the stuff inside. Then we weld a patch on the tank and refill it with gas. Once it crosses to the United States, someone reverses the procedure. It's easy."

"Who else is involved? Who's in charge?"

"I'm going to need your protection," said Harry. "You're going to have to protect me. They'll kill me." Perspiration ran down his face and his thin white fingers clenched and unclenched nervously.

"Don't worry, Harry, we'll protect you," Johnny assured him. "Who's the boss?"

"Helga. Helga runs the whole show."

"Helga?" asked Matthew. "Oh, no!" He was crushed.

"It makes sense," said Johnny. "She has the perfect cover. She'd never be suspected." He turned his tape recorder off. "You've done well, Harry. You can tell me more on the way to town. One other thing...how much heroin are we talking about?"

"You won't believe it," answered Harry. For a split second his sense of pride returned. "More than half a ton."

The blood drained from Johnny's face.

"Is that a lot?" asked Matthew.

Johnny quickly calculated the street value of the drug.

"Worth more than two hundred million dollars on the street. More than the value of all the gold mined during the Gold Rush!"

15

WHERE'S JOHNNY?

For the next twenty-four hours reporters streamed to the Yukon Territory from southern Canada and the United States. Television stations set up mobile satellite transmitters and broadcast the exploits of the Adams children around the world. They were heroes for uncovering the largest drug ring in the history of the North.

"It's crazy out there," sighed Ashley. She was watching the reporters gathered outside their motel room. She and Jonathan were offered money by a newspaper for exclusive rights to their story. A manufacturer of in-line

skates wanted them to endorse their products. Newspapers carried dramatic headlines.

"This is my favorite," said Matthew. *"CALIFORNIA KIDS CLIP KINGPINS!* I like this one, too. *FAST FREDDY AND FRIENDS FOIL FIENDS!* We'll have to save these to show Dad."

"I suspect Dad has seen a few already," said Jonathan.

"Listen to this," interrupted Ashley. She read from a newspaper. "Gang members confessed everything when questioned at R.C.M.P. headquarters in Haines Junction. In a statement released today, the commanding officer congratulated the special task force that conducted the investigation. He said only teamwork could yield such success."

"Do you believe it? They aren't giving Johnny any credit. That stinks."

"Johnny's name isn't mentioned in any stories," said Jonathan. "They change our quotes. They want it to sound like the police force did it with a little help from us. Johnny doesn't even exist."

"They'll probably fire him for disobeying orders," said Matthew. "That's the kind of world it is. Follow the rules or get kicked out. Like Dad says...if you think for yourself, you're always a target."

"Yeah," agreed Ashley. "Then he turns around and teaches us to think for ourselves."

"It doesn't make any sense to me," concluded Matthew.

"Why don't we find Johnny and see what's happening?" suggested Ashley.

"I have a better idea," said Matthew. "Why don't we find Johnny and get him to help us search for the treasure? Would that be excellent, or what?"

Ashley and Jonathan burst out laughing.

"Matt," said Jonathan, "that's a righteous idea."

"Let's find Johnny," said Ashley. "If we find the treasure, we'll *really* have a story."

They went through the bathroom window into the warm summer evening. The reporters didn't see them leave.

"Where do we go?" asked Matthew. "How are we going to find Johnny?"

"We'll ask," said Jonathan. He chose a small, tidy home and knocked on the front door. A pleasant looking man answered.

"Hello, son. Can I help you?" He saw Ashley and Matthew. "Say, aren't you the Adams kids? Come in, come in." He ushered them into the house and introduced himself as Benny.

"Excuse us for disturbing you, sir," said Ashley, "but we need help. We're trying to find Johnny Johnson."

"No problem," said Benny. "I'll gladly help the most famous visitors in the Junction. We'll take my truck." Without asking questions, Benny led them to his pickup.

Jonathan was surprised when Benny turned down a rutted, muddy road. "It looks like we're leaving town. Doesn't Johnny live in town?"

"He lives back a few miles," replied Benny. They soon pulled up at a small cabin. There were no other houses in sight.

Benny rapped on the door.

"Come in...it's open," called Johnny Johnson.

Benny guided the others into the dimly-lit cabin.

"Benny! This is a surprise...what are you doing here?" Johnny was obviously happy to see them. "What's the occasion?"

"We were wondering what's happening to you at work," began Ashley. "They haven't mentioned your name in the papers and your boss is taking all the credit for catching the smugglers. We think it's unfair."

"I appreciate your concern, but I disobeyed orders. I'm suspended pending an investigation. Maybe I'll get fired, but who knows, eh?"

"But you caught the crooks," insisted Matthew. "You figured out where they were. You made them talk. I don't get it."

"As you would say, Matthew, *chill*," said Johnny. "There are ways of doing police work and I broke the rules. When I break the rules, I have to take the consequences."

"We sure had fun, Johnny," said Jonathan. "I hope they don't fire you."

"If you're losing your job," said Matthew, "can you help us find the treasure? If your goose is cooked, it might as well be cooked totally, right?"

"Matthew, when are you going to learn not to..."

Ashley didn't have a chance to finish her question.

"Treasure?" asked Benny. "What treasure?"

Johnny told Benny about the treasure that might be hidden in the cavern at Blarney Creek. When he learned the mysterious shipment might be under water, Benny had an idea.

"I know just the person you need. She belongs to a spelunkers club. They go all over the world just to dive in caves. She lives in Whitehorse and she's the best. I could call her. Should I call?"

"Yes, yes, *yes!*" blurted Matthew. "Ask her if she can come tomorrow, but don't tell her about the treasure."

"Slow down, dude," said Ashley. "Johnny, should we try?"

Johnny's weary face slowly morphed back to the one they all knew. He grinned.

"Rad!" squealed Matthew. "Totally awesome!"

"Here we go again," laughed Ashley and Jonathan.

MATTHEW'S TREASURE

By morning, things were all set. Benny's friend would fly her plane to Gladstone where the others would meet her. She was excited about diving in an unknown cave system.

Johnny borrowed a friend's plane and left Haines Junction at five a.m. with Ashley, Jonathan, Matthew, and Benny aboard. Less than half an hour later they swooped low over Gladstone Lakes and dropped in for a landing. Another plane was already there and Johnny saw a young lady waiting

on shore. She approached as Johnny stepped from his floats.

"Good morning. I'm Vana. Hi, Benny. Did you guys sleep in, or something? I've been waiting half an hour. Where's this mysterious pool?"

"Hi, Vana. I'm Matthew Adams and this is my sister Ashley and brother Jonathan. We found the cave and we need your help to recover the treasure. You look too pretty to dive in caves."

"Well, aren't you the budding little chauvinist?" said Vana, a hint of red rising in her face. "Did they teach you that in school or were you born that way?"

"Chauvinist?" asked Matthew. "What's a chauvinist?"

"You are," answered Ashley.

"Everyone grab a piece of Vana's diving equipment," ordered Johnny. "Handle it carefully. Vana's life depends on it. Benny and I will take the tanks and lights. Let's go."

Carrying the equipment through the dense alders concealing the adit was not easy. Motivated by a common goal, however, they worked as a team. Within an hour they stood at the edge of the black pool of warm water in the center of the cave.

Vana took control.

"This is dangerous. Once I'm in the water, everyone must be prepared to help if something goes wrong. I've never dived without a buddy, so I'm taking a major risk. Pay attention at all times. If I find anything, don't get excited until I'm out of the water. OK?" Vana paused to let her words sink in.

"This looks like an innocent pool," she continued, "but beneath the surface there may be violent currents. This is part of an underground river. There could be miles of caves or it might be only five feet deep. That's why I need the equipment. For instance, see these reels of guideline? I'll let the lines out as I go down and then I can follow them back here. Everyone ready?"

With her dry suit, air regulators, and buoyancy vest, Vana looked more like an astronaut than a diver. Johnny helped her into the water. She slipped below the surface with a splash.

Seconds ticked by and turned into minutes. They waited for Vana's return, hypnotized by the silence and the smooth black water.

"We'll know soon," said Johnny. "I hope you're not disappointed, Matthew. Remember, even if there's no treasure, the journey's been exciting. Having the journey is the greatest reward of all."

"You sound like Dad," said Matthew. "The journey's fine, but treasure would be nice, too."

The pool's surface came to life and Vana's head bolted from the black water. She flipped her mask from her eyes and extended her arm to Johnny. He pulled her from the water.

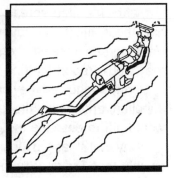

"Did you find anything?" asked Matthew.

Vana reached into a pouch strapped to her waist and withdrew a bar of metal the size of a television remote control. She handed it to Matthew.

He took the object and nearly dropped it. It was heavy!

"Gold," he said quietly, turning the bar in his hands. "It's *gold!* We found real treasure!" He handed the bar to Johnny. "Is it real gold?"

Johnny studied the bar. There was no doubt. "Yes, it's gold...solid gold."

They took turns holding the bar.

"Are there more?" asked Matthew.

"More than we could carry out in a week. There are crates full of these bars. They're all stamped *Property of the United States Government 1944.*"

"What do we do with it?" asked Ashley. "I suppose we have to turn it over to your boss, Johnny. The ultimate insult."

"Treasure!" exulted Matthew. "We solved the riddle and found the treasure! I told you there was treasure, didn't I? I told you!"

Matthew's glee spread to everyone and laughter and high fives filled the cavern, echoing from wall to wall. Vana agreed to salvage one bar for each person and then they would report the find to the authorities.

Benny suggested they call a news conference in Haines Junction and make the announcement. That way they would get to describe the gold discovery themselves.

"Why not?" asked Johnny. "I can't get in any more trouble than I'm already in. Let's go for it."

126

So they did. Pictures of them holding gold bars were flashed around the world. They appeared on magazine covers and were asked to recount their adventures on morning TV programs. After the news conference, Johnny's suspension was lifted and he was put in charge of recovering the rest of the gold.

An investigation revealed the gold had been stolen from the United States Government near the end of the Second World War. The Government decided to spread its gold reserves across the country in case of invasion. A large shipment was sent from New York to Anchorage, Alaska, but it never arrived. A group of men disguised as soldiers hijacked the gold near Haines Junction in 1944. The gold and the men simply disappeared. Because the operation was top secret, the theft was never made public.

The next day Ashley, Jonathan and Matthew met their father at the Haines Junction airport. After escaping reporters, everyone gathered at Johnny's cabin.

"You should be proud of your children, Dr. Adams," said Johnny Johnson. "They're very independent."

"Thank you, Constable Johnson. I'm grateful you looked out for them."

"Dad," asked Matthew, "do we get to keep any of the gold?"

"I don't know what the law says. Each of you should receive recognition for what you did. I hired a lawyer who knows about these things. She's supposed to be the best. She'll look after any claim you might have."

"Where's she from?" asked Ashley and Jonathan at the

same time.

"New York. I spoke with her on the phone. They had to track her down — she was on vacation. She sounds very nice."

The room suddenly became quiet.

"Dad, what's her name?" asked Matthew, his voice shaky.

"Her name? I believe it's Eloise."

Matthew, Ashley, and Jonathan groaned.

"That's the way it goes," laughed Johnny Johnson. "That's just the way it goes."

THE END

About the Author

David Skidd grew up in Eastern Canada and attended St. Mary's University in Halifax, the University of Ottawa, and the University of Kansas. He has taught at universities in the United States and overseas.

An avid reader and writer, David enjoys music, Northern living, and learning about different cultures and philosophies.

In the *Alaska Highway Adventure Series,* David combines mystery and adventure with the natural sense of wonder felt by all who love the North.

About the Cover Artist

Jim Robb is a well known Yukon artist, historian and photographer. In Whitehorse, Mile 918 on the Alaska Highway, Jim's work can be seen in galleries, bookstores, and even on fine china. Jim uses his unique style and humour in depicting past and present life north of 60°.

Jim is busy working on volume Number 3 of *The Colourful Five Per Cent Illustrated,* known to be "read in all the better cabins." He is also developing a cartoon series featuring Northern people and places, and is illustrating stories celebrating the centennials of the discovery of gold (1996) and the Gold Rush (1998).

Jim is a quintessential Yukoner, focusing today's energy on a vision of tomorrow informed by a respect for the past.

The author is grateful for Jim's contribution to this book.